For my dear, Please
Jill & Alex, don't lend this to
ANYONE!!.
I love you,

Richy
1993

January

Peachy

ALSO BY FREDRICA WAGMAN

Playing House
Magic Man, Magic Man

Peachy

FREDRICA
WAGMAN

Published by
Soho Press Inc.
853 Broadway
New York, NY 10003

Library of Congress Cataloging-in-Publication Data

Wagman, Fredrica.
Peachy / Fredrica Wagman.
ISBN 0-939149-72-9
I. Title.
PS3573.A36P4   1993
813′.54—dc20   92-17517
                                                  CIP

Manufactured in the United States
10 9 8 7 6 5 4 3 2 1

For Joel, James, Anne, Nela,
Mary and Nancy Wagman,
and for Ruth Singer

"I have set before thee Life and Death—Choose Life.
Deuteronomy

Peachy

"It's all in the gaze."—*Alfred Marvel*

Chapter

1

I was walking on Brattle Street when I noticed for the first time that I had become invisible. Men kept passing me like I wasn't there. I, who used to make heads spin when I'd walk into any restaurant in Vineland or when I'd mosey down any street in Philadelphia, had suddenly merged into that great wave of shapes that moves along, stops at the light, advances carefully after it changes and then disappears without the semblance of a memory. It was on Brattle Street up in Cambridge, Massachusetts, not far from Harvard Yard, where I noticed that I had become a part of that great vast blur of faces that no one even sees as they go by. That's where I noticed for the first time that I had become part of that big army of bodies that look like they're made of jelly maybe, or maybe they're made of marmalade, but either way, in the end, finally, they appear as nothing more than a huge, gray moving background for life.

"So, Peachy," I mutter as I straighten myself up to my full five feet four, "face it, kid, you're forty-five years old and no eye-catcher anymore."

But, come *on!* Is that really what it's all about? Is the whole entire point of being alive your attraction for the opposite sex? Isn't it supposed to be more like what Flaubert was talking about when he said, "You have to discover your own true nature and then be in harmony with it." He said, "You have to break with the whole outside world, live like a bear and hold onto only your *mind!*" I'm thinking as I stop for a light on the corner of Brattle Street and Mt. Auburn Avenue.

Wish I were home, I'm thinking as I begin walking again.

If I were home I'd be driving Ruthie to school today. . . . All along the highway as far as the eye could see would be endless fields of corn and green shimmering flatlands that sprawl from unpaved winding roads to the horizon flanked by little mountains of pine trees that are always a kind of purple by the end of summer. . . .

But no. The day I realized I had become invisible began in a sea of cars that were crammed into the scorching parking lot of Harvard's Business School. Freshmen like my daughter Ruthie were assigned housing directly across the Charles River in a great walled-in park called Harvard Yard, and the only way to get to it was through that roasting maze of metal where half the kids were puking up their breakfasts beside their parents' rented cars.

But not Ruthie, I'm thinking as I'm walking.

Just her silence.

She never said a word as we inched our way in that long caravan toward the little stone bridge that was just beyond the parking lot.

She never uttered a sound as we drove over it, crossed Massachusetts Avenue and then entered into that great shaded enclave of stately buildings, enormous ancient trees and sprawling overgrown lawns heavy with the last of summer all on them.

She didn't make a sound as we parked in the shade of Stoughton Hall and then, like two little immigrants, we began unloading all her belongings onto the gravel. Not a word as the two of us lugged her trunk up four flights of narrow stairs to a small room that had brick walls, a working fireplace, three big windows set deep inside dark, wooden, shuttered window boxes, and wide oak floors.

Not a word as we hung up all her skirts and put all her underwear, socks and sweaters into the cherry chest of drawers that had a cherry framed mirror on the top. Nor was she able even to say good-bye. She just stood there.

Except for her class trip to the Seaquarium in Miami Beach when she was a senior in high school, she had never been this far from Vineland in her life.

So Harvard University, *Big Deal! Guess What? I'm Not Impressed Because You See This Child Still Belongs To Me! Okay! So Not So Fast With Trying To Suck Her Up Into This Whole Big Fancy Rigmarole You Have Going On Up Here Because This Is Still M Y C H I L D! DO YOU UNDERSTAND? MINE!*

M I N E! M I N E! I start choking exactly as I had done two hours before when we were carrying all the cardboard boxes up those stairs.

Mine! I was seething as I was making her bed. *Mine!* I was gasping as I was putting her shoes away. *Mine!* I was hissing at every tree and bush and every lousy blade of grass in that whole rotten shithole place called Harvard Yard.

The day before we left for Cambridge I watched her from the kitchen window as she was hanging the wash out on the line. The wind was so strong that day that it blew the long blue cotton skirt she was wearing into a kind of cocoon around her legs while her long brown curly hair was flying in her face as the sheets billowed out in front of her like the immense sails of an old-fashioned clipper ship. The weather and the sky weren't summer anymore. That day had that first hint, that first edge, that first something of fall that had begun so imperceptibly it was almost as though a black shadow were passing through the air, and as I stood watching her from the kitchen window I was begging time to stop! *please!* so I could hold onto all of it, to Ruthie and to the sunshine and to the sheets that were billowing in the wind—this! "*THIS!*" I whispered, before it all gets lost to time and taken.

Her childhood was over and I was mourning it as I stood watching her from the window caught in the grip of love and sorrow that suddenly became one feeling that was almost unendurable—You give them death the same as you give them life I was thinking, and that's what was so unbearable. She was eighteen already and I had just turned forty-five. Where had it gone? How long ago since that day in a little park in Vineland where old Leo Fish and I stood watching an ancient Chinese man dressed all in black heaving handfuls of birdseed high into the air. Pigeons were swarming around his head like a living halo as he stood tossing the seed in his little black Mary-Jane shoes, his face radiant with so much joy that I was begging time to stop! *please!* so I could hold onto him, and to that day, and to the sun, and to all the pigeons as I stood beside my father, dumb with so much happiness.

There used to be a hill behind an empty warehouse in Philadelphia where my brother Charlie and I used to play I was thinking as I was sitting on the bare ticking mattress of Ruthie's strange new bed in Stoughton Hall with one of her speaker boxes in my lap, and as I sat there I was remembering how my brother Charlie used to yell at the top of his lungs for me to hurry up. *"Hurry Peachy!"* he'd shriek. "Come *on! Let's go!"* he'd scream at the top of his lungs as we ran to catch the ferry that went from Camden across the river to Philadelphia. Then we'd tear over to our hill, race all the way up to the top, drop all our books and, while Charlie sat up there talking to himself out loud and saluting like an army general, I'd start rolling down the hill, my skirt twisted up above my knees as I was rolling over and over and over myself and the thin coolness of the grass against my cheeks and the sweet smell of summer just beginning and the warmth again and the hope, and as I was rolling I was begging time to *Stop! PLEASE!* so I could hold onto all of it, to the smell of the earth and to the warmth of the sun and to how beautiful it was out there—so ecstatic was I in the flush of a moment that was perfect.

Then back we'd fly to the ferry, me and Charlie, and then back out on the water again past the giant cranes and cargo ships and tugs and steamers and the big rusty freighters anchored in crumbling piers and the gulls out there where the flat stretches of empty marshland thinned down to the water's edge, and me and my brother, and a feeling of pure unsplintered peace which is what freedom is I'm thinking, as Ruthie and I began walking together back down the four long flights of narrow stairs, then out the door and then over to the green Cutlass station wagon we rented in Vineland for the trip.

In silence, all of it.

I got in, pulled the door closed, turned on the ignition and then I reached out the window to take her hand.

Still not a word. Not a sound. Just silent tears boiling down her face as we looked at each other.

Then I withdrew my hand, put the car into gear, released the brake, put my foot on the accelerator and left. When we were children my brother Charlie was always making plans to get away from Vineland, but not me. I never dared have a dream like that. I was the girl, so of course I understood how I'd live my life. I had a mother to take care of—her errands, her ailments, her old age and all her checkups, that was my domain, my territory, in a house not far from hers beside the great, sprawling Pine Barren Forest of New Jersey that goes on and on for mile after mile of low, scrubby, wild evergreens, and the loons in there, and the smell of the earth.

But I had no complaints.

I loved the earth and I always felt I owed it something back. That's what I was thinking as I left Ruthie standing there and started driving toward the big iron gates that protected Harvard Yard from the Massachusetts Avenue side of Cambridge, a town so fiercely energized that you almost couldn't breathe. Wow! So much brain power going on up here I was saying to myself as I wiped my eyes and nose on the back of my hand, drove through the iron gates and then swung the empty green Cutlass station wagon onto Massachusetts Avenue heading toward a parking lot I had seen on Brattle Street.

"Money's everything."—*Alfred Marvel*

Chapter

2

The night before, when we had arrived in Cambridge, immediately after Ruthie and I checked into the Sheraton Commander, I made a plan for the following day.

After I settled her into her dormitory room, helped her unpack and put everything away, and then, after we made all our good-byes, I planned to drive directly to the parking lot on Brattle Street, park the green Cutlass station wagon and then walk the five or six blocks on Brattle Street to WordsWorth discount bookstore which was at the corner of Brattle and Mt. Auburn Avenue. That way, I had decided, there'd be no need to worry about crossing any of those streets that were all torn up or walking aimlessly for hours trying to collect myself and then getting lost if I made even one wrong turn, and since I had such a terrible sense of direction anyhow, my object was to just get to WordsWorth's in one piece, and then, once inside that tunnel system, that labyrinth of aisle after aisle of books on bookshelves where Ruthie and I had poked in our heads the night before, I'd be just another character passing a little time until the storm was past.

But from the look of it, for some of the people who were in there last night, the ones who were leafing through calendars at one in the morning, for them it looked like maybe the storm might never pass. But as I told myself last night, for a person like myself, for a matron in her middle forties with salt and pepper hair cut in a boyish bob, a trim tan poplin Calvin Klein suit with a white silk blouse that has a bow at the neck and Gucci walking shoes, for this type, hopefully, the crisis would only be temporary.

Look, I'm thinking as I'm walking, you can't hold onto a child because holding on isn't love. That's number one. And number two, you've been through a lot worse than this in your life I'm telling myself as I scramble around in my pocketbook for a Kleenex. But okay, so what? So I have, I answer myself. But what good is this kind of thinking? What am I supposed to do? Dwell on all the other sadnesses of my life in order to make this one seem a little easier? I'm thinking as I blow my nose. Look, I tell myself as I start walking again, this time you're losing a child to *Life!* This time it's like the article in the *TODAY* section of the Vineland Ledger said, "You're losing your college age child to the *Future! To Hope! To Advancement!* and *To The Possibility Of Making a Real And Meaningful Contribution.*" And for a second, that second that comes up every now and then like a little cloud that flies across my mind on one small brown translucent wing, my other child, the one who was killed, peers out at me from the numbing blanket of time. . . .

So "Life doesn't let you live," like Aunt Martha Cohen always used to say, but at least there's one thing about being a woman that men don't have to ever worry about, I'm thinking, as I stop for a light and blow my nose again. You sure get a strange reward for a job well done. Ha! Your prize is that one day they get up and walk out the door and that's *that*—Good-bye—See you around—So long! And that's if you're *lucky!* If you aren't so lucky they kick you first and then walk out the door and if you *really* screwed things up, if you really made a big mess out of everything, then they don't walk out the door at all; they just sit around staring at you forever. So of course, I'm thinking as I start walking again, *of course* it's sad when they leave but I always knew it was part of the entire package from the very beginning. So come on, Peachy: What are you complaining about? The subject we're discussing now is *Strength, Peachy—Strength!* It's like what Nietzsche said, *"That which does not kill me only makes me stronger."*

And as I stop for another light my husband Alfred's busty little secretary in her short tight-fitting skirt, her black spiked heels and that hair or whatever it was, that dyed black, lacquered beehive on top of her head made of fiberglass maybe or maybe it was made of nylon filaments, her freckled face and dead white skin and that left eye of hers that turned all the way in, knots up my stomach again for the zillionth time. . . . So what about her too, I'm thinking. What does it mean, what does she mean and what does it matter anyhow? I'm wondering as I pass a tall attractive man, possibly a professor from the looks of his gray tweed jacket, his horn-rimmed glasses and his scruffy salt and pepper beard whom I notice doesn't so much as even move an eyebrow toward me for even a fraction of a second as we pass each other.

That whole man-woman thing is completely nonexistent anymore, I'm thinking as he passes me by as we're walking like I wasn't even there.

So! It's *nothing!* I tell myself, a fluke, that's all. It's not any kind of serious *rejection* I reassure myself as I fluff up my hair. It's just the result of all those *feminists*. These days a man is too damn scared to even *look at a woman* since all those damn women's libbers have begun shouting names if a man so much as even *glances* over so what can we expect, I scoff, as I peer at my face in the window of the Ann Taylor Shop. Even *truck drivers* don't toot as they go pounding down the street anymore thanks to all those damn "liberated" women who, God forbid, should ever use a drop of powder or some lipstick maybe or maybe a little base I'm thinking as I'm rustling around in my bag for my lipstick. So of course a college professor like that man probably was would be the first to resign under any kind of fire I sneer as I apply the creamy mauve grease without benefit of a mirror, so well do I know the outline of my mouth after all these years that it goes on almost by itself. After all, I laugh, those militant little twerps who don't bother to even bleach their moustaches anymore or shave their legs or shave under their arms, God forbid!, are his *bread and butter,* I sneer again, so of *course* he's going to be the first to break down under this kind of feminist pressure I scoff again as I look down in my hand at the little tip of purple lipstick sticking out of its metal tube like the tip of dog's little red thing. And for a second I see Ruthie and all those friends of hers who *all* yell at men instead of being flattered if a guy winks or clucks his tongue. Why? What's so terrible that they should scream that he's some kind of *pig* who should *Go fuck himself shithead* at the top of their voices if he gives a little whistle or does that little clicking sound with his tongue like you do to make a horse go faster. They should be *flattered!* I'm thinking. But no, those little snits, with their wild flying hair and those wobbly boobies they have, give him the finger and holler *Piss off dirtball*. Why? I wonder as I shoot an artistic-type fellow with long blond hair, a trench coat that's all buttoned up with a long sweeping yellow scarf around his neck, a little smile.

Again nothing!

Not so much as even a little *glance* or even one of those terse little nods in my direction that are innocently exchanged between people that asks no price.

Okay! So I just passed another gutless wimp, I comfort myself, another spineless yellow belly who's pathetically trying not to look like the full-blooded male animal he really is as he charges down the street like he has blinders on. *Fine!* "Go right ahead you cowardly jerk," I mutter, as I reach around in my bag for my plastic hairbrush. One of these days I'll have to sit down with all those little feminist friends of Ruthie's so we can discuss why they're so dead set against a harmless little smile in passing or a certain kind of glance that says, You're pretty and yes you have great legs because frankly, girls, I used to love that kind of stuff. But no! Thanks to you, you girls have gone and ruined everything, and maybe for good. But wait a minute! *Excuse me!* I'm not allowed to call you "girls" anymore, am I? I have to say *women!* So pardon me! I scoff. So now thanks to you they rape, mug and strangle us instead of whistling and making little clucking sounds, and if that isn't bad enough, the judges stand behind those lunatics *one million percent!* (The next attractive man passes me without his eyes so much as even rising for an instant from the air in front of him, only this time I avert my eyes myself.). . . . Those damn lousy judges. *Ha!* I sneer as I fluff up my hair again. They not only do *not* punish all those lunatics who go around raping, mugging and strangling women like there's no tomorrow—are you *kidding?* Those vile women-hating judges put armies of lunatics right back on the streets without so much as a tap on the wrists! And why? Because those vile women-hating judges want all those rapists to keep it up. Keep up the good work, you guys! That's the message. Get back out there and get all the women you want, the judges whisper behind their hands instead of sending those madmen up the river for life. *But no!* Somebody has to show all these hot-shot bitches a thing or two—*right?* the judges whisper. Somebody has to let these hot-shot bitches know who still wears the pants around this country, so lunatics of the world go back out there on the streets and *rape, mug and murder women all you want!* Do you *hear?* How dare they give us the finger for winking or hooting, the judges are all whispering. Somebody's got to show these little bossy bitches that we as men won't take any more of their *nonsense!* Just because we tell them in passing that they have great legs or that we love their boobs, that's when they start yelling back like the house is on fire. Where do they get off calling us *slimy shithead pigs* just because we make a little click at them or make a little kissing sound or holler "reba reba" as they walk by. So just remember, since we've still got the ding-dongs and since we don't want anybody to forget that, Go back out there, the judges whisper, and bash their heads against the sidewalk if you feel like it. Threaten them at knife point just like you did to Ruthie's little friend Leslie Monroe. Remember her? The tennis champ who walked in on two boys who were in the middle of burglarizing her house, so she got raped at knife point from both of them. Or what about Judy Demitritofsky who got murdered trying to fight off the janitor in her apartment building. Or what about that brainy little Betty Marie Jones who was napping in a hammock on her *own front porch* when she was raped and then slashed across the face with a hunting knife. So *bravo!* the judges applaud. Needless to say I stand behind all you monster madmen *one million percent* because we cannot, and I say *cannot*, let any of these little what-ever-the-hell-they-think-they-are flaunt all that hot-shot liberation nonsense in *our* faces. Protect women? Don't make me *laugh!* the judges all are roaring as I come to the corner of Brattle Street and Story where I stop to take a long hard look at the face that's staring back at me from the reflection in the glass window of the Crate and Barrel Shop.

Wow! I'm thinking.

White wild hairs, the first ones to come in, the first har-bingers of women turning into monsters, are zigzagging out of my black boyish bob like little fingers beckoning to me from the grave. My face is all wizened up like a white raisin or like a thumb that's been soaking in a cup of water all day long with black lines going from my nose all the way down to the corners of my mouth like arrows. My *God!* I think as I touch them, they look like somebody carved them in with a pearl-handled pocketknife. And my cheeks, I'm thinking, if I could even refer to them as cheeks anymore, those planes that old Leo Fish used to say looked like I had marshmallows stuffed in them are all sunken now with two beady close-set little pitch black eyes peering out at the world from my accordion-pleated eyelids over a bulbous nose that looks like a swollen strawberry at the end of a stick.

What's happened to my looks, I'm wondering as four luscious young girls walk past as I'm standing there examining each of my shapeless nostrils in the glass reflection, four beauties with loosely slung navy sweaters tied around their waists, white T-shirts over their big wobbly boobs, tight blue dungarees that look like they have God knows what crusted into the crotches, dirty white sneakers, thick white socks, enormous black leather shoulder bags and that look on all their faces, that special happy expectant look that carries with it *Creation and Life!* And as I turn to follow them with my eyes, for a moment, just one moment, I see one of them, the tall one with the reddish hair, stark naked on a little dormitory cot coming like mad with her head hanging over the side of the bed for such a long time, minutes maybe as her boyfriend bangs away all stiff and hard with that look on his face that young men have, that hot disheveled look of something even greater than his own enormous pleasure. It's that passion look that never cares how many times he makes her come, again and again and again in all that blackness, till he bucks and pounds like a mountain tumbling all its rocks, hot lava filling up and spilling down her thighs and then he lets her go as I stand there thinking that just once like that and then she'll be able to pod the peas and dust the mantle and clean and wash and stack, then she'll be able to kiss the children who keep crying and tugging and digging into her, then she'll be able to laugh and sleep and dream. . . . All the oysters of the world are tight within their own hard shells waiting, waiting for just one drop of precious seed to start them making wondrous pearls, yet how many oysters ever get it and what it must be like when they do I'm thinking as I watch them turn the corner laughing at something one of them has said.

Youth all by itself is so astonishingly marvelous. Just that young estrogen thing coursing through the bloodstream of even ugly girls, even girls with nothing to redeem them at all have all it takes—their *hormones!* I'm thinking as I start walking again in the direction of WordsWorth's discount bookstore, which looms ahead of me in the distance like my own private convalescence home.

"Never look back."—*Alfred Marvel*

Chapter

3

My plan was to slip in there unobserved, go all the way to the back of the store, find a corner that would be cool, dark and empty, sit down quietly on the floor, take off my shoes, lean back against the wall, assume the lotus position, take a few deep yoga breaths, do a few neck-relaxing exercises and slowly try to recover.

Another reason why I decided on WordsWorth discount bookstore, beside the fact that it was perfect in terms of just getting there from the parking lot, was that the night before when Ruthie and I were squashed in there for those couple of minutes I was suddenly struck by how closely it resembled the Raymond J. Thorpe Free Library that wasn't far from the old Vineland High School. Maybe it was the same drywall feeling or maybe it was the intensity of so many books all crammed and stuck and piled together without much air, or maybe it was the cheap neon lighting in the ceiling, but for whatever reason, WordsWorth's struck a chord that made me want to get back to see if maybe I'd feel that same euphoria I used to feel so long ago. I was almost Ruthie's age when libraries and certain bookstores produced in me a kind of ecstacy that used to make me almost faint from over-stimulation, and I wanted to feel that feeling again. I wanted that luminous fall like Alice had that went all the way down through time, then back I'd go to the Sheraton Commander, gather up all my belongings and leave for home.

That Ruthie was going to be fine was clear I was thinking as I crossed Mt. Auburn Street. She had everything she needed as far as material things were concerned like blankets, sheets, money and good warm winter clothes. That was all taken care of so no, it couldn't be anything like that that made me start gulping back a whole new wave of tears. No, it was more the thought that she'd have pain, that she'd have to suffer in parting from me the same as I was suffering in parting from her that was so terrible. But the fact is, I told myself as I stopped for the final light, this is how life is and now is as good a time as any to get used to it. The fact is, she does have to suffer like all the rest of us and the fact is, she does have to go through what every bug and bird and every crawling mammal on this planet has to go through. But that thought, the thought that she has to endure the same torture that I endured and that my mother endured and that my grandmother endured before her was unbearable.

Somehow you think *your* child will be exempt from that kind of pain, only your child isn't exempt from anything and that's the killer. It's like what Marty Raintree, the old man who used to clean my grandfather's chicken coops used to say, "We're born alone, we live alone and we die alone." All we are is a little kernel deep inside a crystal ball that's spinning through time all by itself and the whole trick is to find out how to stand the aloneness.

"How!" I mutter out loud as I wipe my nose and eyes on the cuff of my jacket as a couple of good-looking young fellows, probably students from the looks of them, brush past me as though I'm invisible—my suit, my shoes, my hair, even my makeup that's been applied with perfection amounts to zero. Only this time, as they pass, a strange notion begins to form out of that deep murky subterranean fish tank I tote around with me called my brains. Maybe I'm thinking, just maybe it has nothing whatsoever to do with all that hot-shot woman's liberation business, it begins to dawn on me. Maybe I'm thinking, I'm not someone who's worth looking at anymore. Maybe, I'm thinking, I'm slipping, and if that's the case, who am I if I'm not who I always was? And I stop dead in my tracks.

Once, and not so long ago, I used to get stares from men without having to even bat an eye so if I'm not that person anymore, who am I then? If I used to be a decent-looking, attractive woman with enough confidence to have dared to imagine when I was young that I could have convinced Hitler to completely change the way he thought about the Jews if I only had a chance to talk to him, if I used to go out for walks just to hear all those truck drivers on Route 555 shout and honk at me and offer me rides and not just once in a while either, *but all the time!* I was never any kind of raving beauty, but I did have a certain je ne c'est quoi—a certain mystery something despite the fact that my bust was too big and my legs were too short and bowed but nobody ever seemed to mind those things. Men always had that certain blank goofy look on their faces when they looked at me which they did *all the time*. So if I'm not that person, then who am I, I'm wondering, as another man brushes past me without so much as even the smallest glance.

It feels like I'm a ghost, I think, as I start walking across the street, because on the one hand it feels like I'm still alive and yet on the other, because I've become invisible, it feels also like I'm dead. And what's even worse I'm thinking, in the next stage of my life men will begin to see me as just a nuisance. I'll be someone they have to move around, wait until I pass, pardon themselves angrily if I get in their way or feel a general annoyance if I, the old biddy, keeps them waiting for even half a second. You've had it, kid, I begin to understand as I'm walking. Forget them ever giving me a hand again if I want to fill my gas tank at the self-service island—those days are *gone* my friend along with all those traffic tickets I never got that I deserved for crashing through changing lights or making lefts into oncoming traffic. All that's finished! Done! Kaput! "Face it Peachy," I mutter as I nod my head in agreement, "you're turning into an old bat whom they secretly *detest*." And what's more and what's worse by far, they *detest* us because they're afraid of us, because to them we are *monsters* when we get old. You can see it as plain as day in the way their eyes shift all around when they have to look at an old lady. Impatience, that's what it is. Notice the way they talk in a nasty impatient hurry when an old lady asks a question. Face it, slowly that lovely Patricia Fish Marvel who was once the toast of Vineland New Jersey has passed from being a lovely, exciting and admired woman into becoming a mean old bat! a lady policeman-type, a stepmother or an old-maid schoolteacher, which translates into turning into something sexless, I'm thinking as I walk down the three granite steps of WordsWorth's, push open the glass doors and enter the bookstore. You're becoming someone they openly despise and that's *that!* And my heart begins beating harder with anxiety as I make my way past the rows of books straight to the back of the store where it's cool and empty, and as I search out my little spot that's almost near the stockroom door and start to unbutton my jacket and push off my shoes the tears well up again.

Oh well, I whisper as I slither down to the floor. But as I push off my shoe it suddenly dawns on me like a light that all of a sudden is flashing on and off—*Wait a minute!*—*Women are valiant courageous incredible creatures who don't even begin to realize how marvelous they really are! . . .* They are *altruistic, loving, peacemaking champions of decency and kindness. . . .* They give *Life, Love* and *Tenderness nonstop* and all they ask in return is that *the people whom they care about will flourish* so what kind of old bat *monster* is that?

And as I assume the full lotus position, close my eyes, take in a deep yoga breath, open my eyes, and begin to rotate my head in a slow circular motion to begin the neck relaxation exercise I was taught in my yoga class, my eyes are oddly drawn like magnets to the dark far left corner where I notice that I'm being watched by someone who's half-hidden behind the top of a row of books.

It's a man.

I can make out a bald head with big tufts of hair above the ears that look like two fat graying Brillo pads, black bushy eyebrows like wire brushes, a big hook nose which looks more like the beak of a young eagle than a normal human nose, intense, black, piercing eyes, with a finger—it looks like his fore-finger—pressed just above his upper lip as he's watching me.

Hm-m-m-m I'm thinking. Not a sound, not a cough, no clearing his throat or anything. Not even a blink of an eyelid. Oh well, I'm thinking, this is Cambridge alright! On the corner of Massachusetts Avenue in front of the subway station yesterday when we were crossing Brattle Street I saw a half-naked man in green tights, red suspenders, no shirt, chaps and cowboy boots yelling at the top of his lungs that he was the son of the Lone Ranger while hordes of people passed by who looked anything but *normal!* The getups and the attires were *unbelievable!* It was a parade of young and old hippies, offbeat bohemians and one strange-looking fellow with slick greasy hair who looked to me like he was completely green including even his skin. No one warned me how overrun this town is with so many *weirdos.* This whole place is extremely peculiar I'm thinking as I extend my legs all the way out in front of me, smooth my skirt, lean my head all the way back to the wall and close my eyes. "Alfred," I whisper, "Where are you?" and my eyes well up.

"Stay away from people who make you feel lousy."
—*Alfred Marvel*

Chapter

4

We were married in the fall when all the leaves were tossing up their color and their life to the deep blue skies. Apple trees along the roads were full to bursting with their heavy crimson fruit. Indian summer then, with giant paper-looking flowers blooming wild across a fence, zinnias, I think they were. I took a leaf and pressed it in my book, it still holds its shape in some little flaky shadow of that autumn when everything was all brand new. How crisp the earth seemed then like a newness that was somehow deep within the heart of death, winter, coming out of deep warm wine drunk mornings right under our window with little tile roof tops and flower boxes. Holland, remember, the double bed with the satin comforter rolled at the end. Spring in Amsterdam that year, God how long ago, with all those tulips. He bought a whole railroad car of yellow ones. And foggy dawns and haze and nights that were never completely dark, in beds that were always waiting for us as we flew along in his little car that had a windshield that went all the way down, we made love like the oceans and the tides. We slept and woke and found each other. There was a man inside my sheets, a big red-headed man stretched out asleep beside me who always wanted me then, no end to how he wanted me all the time, his hands always grabbing till it got on my nerves even with his sweet warm breath on my cheek, only I don't understand why they call it making love because what did love have to do with it inside those sheets that old lady made who was almost a hundred in that awful light where she sewed in that milk brown room with all those cats she had and that ratty sewing machine and all those yards and yards of such exquisite Egyptian cotton spilling all across the chair, which I used to wrap around me while he slept, wondering if it showed, that a man had been inside my bed and sheets. Inside inside. Tell me, Alfred, did it show as I came down the stairs or when I sat with you in the lobby, that sweet funny smell that was heavy like vapor. God, I could smell it in my hair and on my hands and all over my face and I could even almost see it, too, in the color of my cheeks like a coating or a varnish, with the race always back to bed and that smell again coming up soft and strong and the way it lingered on your big red hairy chest with the window never opened more than a crack in that yellow light and how the room was always a little yellow, too, like his skin after he was done.

Then he'd fall asleep and the rust color of his hair and all that rusty fuzz all over him had turned a little yellow too, the flush gone out of everything till finally everything was yellow with his hand on my breast and not a trace left in him, not a whisper or a wish or anything. And then I'd take his hand away and I'd creep out from beneath his heavy arm that was like a log and then I'd stand in front of the mirror and I'd put my hands on my breasts and feel myself to know the way I felt to him and then I'd run my hands across my belly and feel my bony shoulders and pull on my hips a little and then I'd look at my feet that were exactly like old Leo Fish's feet. Such a weird genetic camera that snaps replicas over the millennia duplicating his feet so perfectly and his nose and his lips just like mine and then, bingo, there was old Leo Fish welded onto my face and onto the end of my legs forever in that same identical nose and lips and feet like his.

Behind all the satin slips with all that lace around the bottom and all the dresses that fell just right across the breasts and shoulders, behind all that scarlet polish on my toenails and every satin bra I ever owned and all that thick black kohl I used to smear around my eyes and all those dabs of pink rouge and creamy peach I'd put like I was Rembrandt on my shiny olive face, behind the smile I shot him on the street that day, a perfect stranger standing there in his big brown coat waiting for the light to change and all the time grinning and giving me the eye alright, with his eyes bulging completely out of his head when he looked at my bust, with that big happy grin of his that he was flashing me so that I could see every tooth in his head, the molars and everything, as I was on my way to the Raymond J. Thorpe Free Library where I was hiding out like I had been doing for a couple of weeks by then after they kicked me out of school, behind all that stupid conversation he started up with me on the street while his eyes were glued to my bust, Boy! His eyes were popping out of his head when he looked at my bust, behind his eyes and behind his khaki pants and that gray tweed jacket he wore and that big brown overcoat of his as we stood together at the traffic light, two total strangers sparring to see what was going on, beneath all his thick red curly hair sticking out of the top of his head like sagebrush with his red freckled face and his hot pink ears and his orange neck and those small blue eyes of his that made him look like a flaming sunset, beneath his neck jerk that yanked his chin clear out of the top of his collar when he got a little nervous when he asked me if I wanted to have a little bite of lunch with him, behind all that awful awkward embarrassment I was feeling so bad I could hardly look at him as I slipped into the booth of the Circle Diner while he flicked his lighter up to my cigarette, behind our little lunch that day and all the coffee and all the cigarettes and the strain when I had to get up the nerve it took to look him dead in the eye, were our babies. That was what was behind all of it. Nancy first, and then came Ruthie ten years later, in soft little pink layettes and music box mornings with a yellow linoleum rug and sunshine dancing on the windowsills I'm thinking as my eyes fill up.

And as I open them and begin rotating my head, and as I pull my shoulders up to my ears and hold them there to the count of five and then as I wipe my eyes on the back of my hand, out of the trail of my eye I see the character behind the bookcase, his eyes still not budging as he's staring at my face with his forefinger still pressed against his upper lip as he's watching me.

Almost half an hour, I'm thinking as I glance at my watch. *Hm-m-m-m*.

And I close my eyes again.

This time I decide to try *counting* myself away from so many distracting thoughts. If I could get myself down to what Yogi Rahashamashi calls our Alpha Center, that's a place he says, where relaxation, creativity and the essence of all joy emanates, then maybe—*maybe!*—I would stand a chance of recovering myself enough to even think about the long drive home. According to Yogi Rahashamashi, who teaches our antistress seminar at Landis High every Tuesday night, first you count backwards from ten to one very slowly and between every three numbers you have to talk yourself into a semihypnotic trance by saying, "Deeper, deeper, I'm going deeper, deeper and deeper." Then I'm supposed to count "ten, nine, eight," and whisper, "Relax, Peachy, relax," and it can't be any halfway effort either. I really have to concentrate. And then, just as I begin to go a little limp, I have to whisper, "Deeper, deeper and deeper," and as I begin to feel the first waves of energy leaving my arms and shoulders I'm supposed to lower my head as I move on to the next step which is to imagine something extremely beautiful, so I think about my mother.

She's singing to me about the blue-gray times that break through for just a second's worth of sweetness. She and I are standing near a little silver pond where lullabies hang like shiny Christmas balls on beautiful little pines as she's singing her heart out to me. She's wearing a white fur coat and little silver shoes and she has a silver ribbon in her hair that's studded with a million sequin beads with her soul smashed all across her face as she holds my hand the way she did right after the baby was killed when we went together for the first time back out to the cemetery that afternoon after the frozen snows had melted, and the ancient ground was hard enough to stand on once again.

"Welcome to the real world otherwise known as corruption."—*Alfred Marvel*

Chapter

5

"Ah-em-m-m," I hear from behind the bookcase. "*Ah-em-m-m, ah-em-m-m,*" I hear again. But as I open my eyes and look over, it doesn't appear that he's made so much as even a peep. He's not doing anything and nothing's changed. He's still just staring at me with his forefinger still pressed tightly against his upper lip.

Okay, I start rotating my head again. If you're some kind of doozy, I'm thinking as I start all over again from scratch with my shoulder-raising exercises, that's fine with me, but please, you live your life and I'll live mine, okay? If you won't bother me I won't bother you. Let's just abide together peacefully like the gray nurse whales and humankind, each doing the other no harm, as Cousteau said on Channel 39. I glare at him as I drop my head forward and start counting backwards all over again. . . . Ten, nine, eight. . . .

My friends with their sunglasses pop up behind my closed eyelids. They're sitting at the club, all day by the pool, with something *done* and yet still dangerous about them, failure written into the finger without the wedding band. But not for Ruthie's generation, not anymore, which is a big plus. In fact, for her generation it's probably just the opposite. It's probably a failure for them to *get* married without having struck out for at least a little while on their own. But for a *man!* For any *putz* under the sun there's no such thing as failure, wedding ring or no wedding ring, as long as he has that thing between his legs, little or big, hard or soft, it doesn't matter, it's just like they say, When a husband dies the wife is a widow but when a wife dies, the husband is a prince who just keeps playing golf like he always did and going to the office and coming home whenever he pleases, never looking to see what time it's getting to be until one day, just like that, the time has all run out! *Done!* Because sooner or later everything is done no matter what you do or don't do, like sooner or later everything dries up, the spot on your skirt, the cornfields, the laundry, your skin, and then you look around and they're gone, too, Ruthie and all her precious little friends, all those little girls we watched growing up, their childhoods: Done! Boom! Just like that. A single season, that's all it was while I keep getting older and older next to all the china plates my mother gave me and all her old lace tablecloths waiting for the sweats to start. I hear all our sex glands shrivel up into one big angry knot and all the million little eggs that were half of all the babies we never had but carried around in our ovaries from the first day of our lives or even earlier, dry up too, just like that, making us a walking crematorium for approximately one hundred million people whom we never had but could have which is why we get those hot flashes.

My mother used to lie across her bed fanning herself and patting eucalyptus oil softly into all the folds around her eyes, something about eternal youth. She used to wear those little housecoats that were sort of short sporty floral robes with her arch-support shoes and her stockings rolled down to the ankle and her girdle underneath, her harness that came down from her bust to the top of her thighs with all those bones in that hideous color that's supposed to look like flesh that she never took off night or day. Always walking fast, click click click, her heels on the hardwood floor or in the kitchen or on the street, with her black hair net and her starched white separate cuff or collar sets for all those navy blue wool dresses she used to wear, click click click on the street so fast.

What was the big hurry Hendella? Tell me, I'm thinking, as I let my head roll all the way back to the wall remembering how, when I was a child, grown-up women used to dazzle me. I'd be dumbfounded staring at them, stunned by their size and mystery and sex.

"*Ps-s-st*," I hear. "Hey! *Ps-s-s-st, ps-s-s-st. You!*" I hear him hissing.

Oh, come *on*, I'm thinking as I open my eyes. Leave me *alone!* I have things to think about—*okay?* I shoot him a filthy look.

. . . Ten, nine, eight—deeper, deeper, I'm thinking, you're going deeper, deeper, deeper.

"Relax, Peachy, relax!" I'm whispering to myself as Alfred

pops in, this time on his sailboat *THE PEACH*. We're heading for the open sea, he and I, on some boundless trip that has no end like we vowed on our wedding day when my hair was way down, long past my shoulders, while the old Negro man brought in the drinks and took away the ladies' coats with real gardenias floating in a crystal bowl and flickering candles that made long eerie shadows all across my grandmother's old lace tablecloth with all the people we invited nodding in all their fancy clothes, their puppet strings beginning to get all tangled up in each others' strings. All those people who used to laugh at things that weren't funny, while I cut off all my hair just so I could let it grow again which was how I marked the years by the inches of my hair growing in or very short again, six inches to my shoulders, and then it would be Christmas, the snow would lie in drifts along the road, the air would be bitter cold with such black long nights until the spring again when my hair would be way down below my shoulders so of course I'd have to cut it off again and wait until it grew, like something important was always happening. Alfred used to say that boredom was simply not being able to express yourself but I never agreed with that or with a lot of things that he or his sister Simone had to say.

My *God!* what a pickle that one was! Just like his father, little Moses Marvel, in all his belligerent silences and that mother of his and all her narrow corridors she used to try to squeeze me into so I would become like all of them, my *God!* she tried to make me take the shape of the Queen of Hearts, all upside-downside with nothing real to chew. She tried to seal me up in there with purple sealing wax till it was spring again, when my hair would be real long again, so I could cut it off, and then begin waiting, waiting, while another year and then another after that rolled out of winter with a big pink breath and a shrug.

I think my mother would rather have seen me married than have seen me happy and I went along which is the weirdest part just like she went along and just like Granny Heinfling went along, without a peep, while all the skinny women in their sunglasses kept coming back to sit around the pool out at the country club jabbering all the time about what fools they are for men as they'd nibble on their chicken slices neat on toast with all the crusts cut off and never a drop of mayonnaise and never, never touch a drop of sugar—which was their whole story like money was to their husbands—thin and money to distract them from the fact that one day they'd be dead. Most marriages are somewhere between slavery and prostitution unless the woman has some money herself I used to think as I watched them dab their lips and put their napkins in their laps with their matching bags and shoes just right and they always hid their little watches inside a little golden door that had a snap to get a peek at the time of day it happened to be getting on to with nothing left except to shun dessert and maybe take a nap. . . .

"Hello, Mr. Mingo," I'd hear him saying before my eyes were open in the morning as he was standing by the telephone in his six-hundred-dollar bathrobe that was piped in gold and his black velvet Gucci bedroom slippers and that big fancy leather belt he wore with the looping double Gucci G's for the buckle. With the receiver cradled between his chin and his shoulder, he'd walk across the room lighting a cigarette, then he'd yank up the venetian blinds so abruptly I'd be in shock from so much sudden light as I'd hear, "Listen, Mr. Mingo, I'm looking at approximately two hundred cases of the best Russian sable pelts you ever laid eyes on in your *life!* They are *exactly* the color of Mrs. Mingo's hair," he'd blast as he lit another cigarette. "I can give them to you for four thousand dollars because just now I'm a bit over-inventoried, so you'll make out like a bandit if you take them off my hands before I have my orange juice. Mr. M.," he'd mutter deep into the telephone. "You'll get the deal of the century, take my word for it," he'd begin to whisper on the sly like he had a gun to Mr. Mingo's brain, then his voice would take a very sneaky turn, something low-key and shifty would take over whenever he was selling Leopold Mingo Russian sable pelts.

"Look, Mr. Mingo," he'd whisper as he lit another cigarette, "four thousand dollars for the lot is what I said and that's *what I mean!* I'm not getting into bed with you for one penny less. *Ha! Ha! Ha!*" he'd fake laugh. "No, I don't drop my pants so fast with pelts like this, Mr. Mingo." Alfred would fake laugh again into the telephone as he'd walk back in a trance to the night table drawer to get his Stimudents. I'm remembering, as I open my eyes and begin digging around in my bag for a pack of Kleenex and then, as I shoot a glance over to see if the character with the Brillo-pad hair is still back behind the bookcase watching me, which he is, I wipe my eyes and blow my nose.

As far as fur brokers went, Alfred was probably the biggest in the world. And as far as wholesale furriers went, which translated means an extremely good customer, Leopold Mingo was maybe the biggest wholesale furrier in the world. Sables! Rabbits! Mink! Weasel! Squirrel! Ermine! Chinchilla! Kolinsky! Nothing was too good, too cheap, too expensive, too crappy or too old and stinking from years of camphor storage to "stick on some dumb schmuck," Leopold Mingo used to laugh.

At eighty-seven he not only had all his marbles but he still saw hookers twice a week at five hundred dollars a shot, whores who, to his way of thinking, were the key to the whole fur industry. Whenever his buyers came to New York, Mr. Mingo's hallmark was to supply each of them with a deluxe suite at the Sherry Netherland complete with a gorgeous girl in bed and all ready to go, a black one if that was what the buyer from Des Moines was looking for, a Chinese girl if that was what the head of Greenhammer Hicks in Wichita wanted, two at a time for the old Kraut from Philips Carson in Minneapolis and always three at once for the buyer of the Drimbau chain, Doug March, who called himself "the Machine." And no one had to even pick up a phone. Leopold Mingo would simply slide their room key across the table when their fabulous dinner was over and then wink and nod indicating that it was all taken care of— *Everything!*

In his palatial apartment on Park Avenue swamped in a collection of art treasures that were all museum quality, Chagalls, Soutines, Matisses and great chunks of dark green Rodins that could rip open the hearts of even the most greedy, cold-blooded savage, there was a small alabaster girl attached to a tall mahogany pedestal with a revolving base, a girl that was so icy white, so smooth and exquisite that I wanted to lick her legs or suck on her head for a second as she stood at the top of a little alabaster staircase. The stone was so translucent white and fascinating that it seemed like the stone itself was death. It was so otherworldly and magical that the minute Alfred went out to take a leak, Mr. Mingo, who noticed my excitement, escorted me by my elbow over to the girl to have a better look. Then with his bulging eyes and eyeglasses that were three inches thick glued to the powder room door he spun the base real fast sending the alabaster girl whirling round and round and as she whirled he grabbed my breast in one hand and my face in the other as he jammed his tongue down my throat while his beefy bulging eyes behind his three-inch eyeglasses kept scanning the powder room door like a radar screen.

"Those Chinese bastards have the best red fox, the best mink and maybe the best rabbit in the world," he told Alfred at dinner an hour later, "but what can you do with them? They're so unpredictable! No incentive—True?"

"True," Alfred answered, as he leaned all the way back in his gilded dining room chair and lit a huge cigar. "Either they hike their price or they drop their price so fast it makes your head spin just from reading those stinking cablegrams. True?" Alfred asked.

"Chinese torture," Mr. Mingo answered, as I felt his hand inching up my thigh under the table. "After all," he said as he began pressing with all his might against my arm, "what do they care?" he laughed. "It's socialism's problem, not theirs—right? They're only the keepers, they're not the owners, so what difference does it make to them?" he laughed again. "And those

Russkies aren't any better," he smirked. "Granted they have the best sable and broadtail money can buy, but you still can't do any business like you can't do business with those damn stinking Indians either," he rambled on as he kept pushing with all his strength against my hand.

It was his strength I'm remembering, that dried up old bone was made of steel. At eighty-seven years old he was pure gristle, energy and force.

Then, as the chocolate cake was being served by a dapper mulatto in a cut-away, Mrs. Mingo—a kind of fine-boned relic preserved into her antiquity by the riches of life and wearing jewels I had never seen anything like even in magazines, rubies and diamonds in her ears, a huge ruby and diamond cluster clip with great chunks of uncut cabochon emeralds hanging in chains against her pale satin blouse—leaned over to take my other hand as she whispered sweetly that this particular chocolate cake had won her mother the supreme reputation of being one of the finest hostesses in Chattanooga where she, Iris Mingo, had come from over sixty years before, she oozed graciously, as she clutched my hand warmly, while under the table her husband was pushing against my left arm with the force of a bulldozer.

"Ah, those cow-eyed Sikhs in their pink turbans and their three-piece suits," he laughed as he proposed a toast with his free hand just to make what he was doing under the table even more deceitful. And as the deep red claret wallowed just below the faceting of his Baccarat cut-crystal wine glass, turning the light that hit it into fiery blues and oranges that danced on the air like bits of wild diamond dust, his fierce hand, as though it weren't attached to anything in the room, this thing that shot out of Mr. Mingo's jacket like a wild savage that had a life of its own kept pushing toward my underpants.

"Oh come *on!*" I hear Alfred laughing cozily. "Those Indians are the worst bastards that ever walked the earth!" he laughed as he sipped his claret.

"Remember Hagi Lamont Singh?" he asked Mr. Mingo. "Do you remember how that stinking son of a bitch used to get so sloshed at my house he'd pass out cold on the toilet and how it took two people, usually me and my houseman Crump, to drag him up the stairs. Never mind the forty hand-carved tiny ivory elephants that come in a minuscule ivory button. Forget the blue sari for Peachy or that black mother-of-pearl inlaid jewel box with all the silver bangle bracelets inside for Ruthie, and the yards and yards of the most beautiful silk I ever saw, white with gold brocade and black with silver. Because in those crates," Alfred said, "along with the best muskrat pelts you've ever seen, Hagi was shipping ten-pound bags of heroin valued at approximately five million dollars—that's right! Crank! Horse! Or as they call it in my old neighborhood, 'The Big Uncle!'

"Every month, just like clockwork it came to a certain person on the shipping platform at my warehouses in Newark," Alfred said, as he was trying to relight his huge Havana cigar, "and this person got it to another person in the bookkeeping department in the Passaic office, whose sister was the chief switchboard operator at New Jersey Utilities Incorporated, and this switchboard operator got it to every casino in Atlantic City."

"You don't mean it," Mr. Mingo commented, as his hand, like one of those iron masts that holds up the Brooklyn Bridge, was at a stalemate three inches from my crotch.

"That's right," Alfred went on, "the same Hagi Lamont Singh who used to dance around our living room with an upside-down broom so abandoned and moved by the friendship, booze, cigarettes and feelings of well-being that sprang up between us that his eyes would roll all the way back and tears would appear as he waltzed the broom silently around our living room. But did he ever say a word about the two of us being in the heroin business together? Did he ever give one hint that such a thing was possible, no less that it was *happening* month after month, year after year under the finest muskrat pelts that money could buy. And what's more, *he was charging me the freight!* The fucking bloodsucker was taking me to the *cleaners* on the freight bills alone while he was risking my *life!* my livelihood and my reputation. And that's not to mention *the Evil,*" Alfred says.

. . . But Alfred was a real innocent, I'm thinking, as I remember the look on his face the night that Hagi Lamont took off his turban, long before Alfred knew anything about the heroin, and *that* made Alfred buy the whole man.

"Do you know what it MEANS for a Sikh to take off his *turban, Peachy?*" he asked me, so excited he was almost shaking. So of course he wouldn't let Hagi take it off until he returned the honor by dashing downstairs to get a bottle of his best Möet Blanc de Blanc champagne to honor the occasion because, he whispered to me while he was driving in the corkscrew, "Everybody knows that sikhs *never* take them off *for anyone!* It's the most private thing, sort of like me pulling down my underpants," he whispered as Ruthie and I stared wide-eyed at what was going on under Hagi's turban.

We were gaping with our mouths wide open and mostly because of his beard that had been separated at the chin and then pulled up tight along both sides of his face all the way to the top of his head where it was made into a big fat bun which he told us he had never cut in his entire life. Not one hair on either his head or face had ever been so much as snipped or shortened, which meant that every hair from the day he was born was tied up into one of the maybe twenty little knobs on the top of his head with the fat beard-bun in the center. It was incredible to see him as he sat on the edge of the bed in the guest room with his pink turban in his lap, his face mellow in a rush of love that seemed to envelop his whole enormous countenance.

But the gesture was as hollow as the man I'm thinking. Since he had no conscience, everyone around him eventually got hurt only we didn't know that then. Then we toasted all his knobs and buns, "*Hooray!*" as he was wildly pulling them loose so he could show us how long it all had gotten over his entire lifetime. There's something fascinating about hair—we were spellbound as we watched it flying all over, his soft fluffy mane, so next we drank to how much hair he had. His hair and his beard came down all the way past his waist. "Hooray!" we shouted as we toasted Mahatma Gandhi and Hagi's eyes filled up.

"He vas dee must beautiful man dat ever *lived!*" he shouted.

Then we toasted George Washington just to be fair. "*Hooray!*"

Then we toasted Ruthie Marvel who had just gotten into every college she applied to. "Hooray for Ruthie Marvel" we all were shouting while Hagi was so juiced up by then he could barely walk as we made our way out of the house, across the driveway and then over to the apple orchard behind the garage, our arms looped around each other's waists while Hagi began chanting ancient Indian melodies with tears rolling down his cheeks while Alfred, who was also juiced up pretty good himself was sobbing like a baby as he began digging a hole in the earth so he could bury the bottle of champagne next to the grave of our old cat Perry who got run over by the milkman two months before. The buried champagne was to be a monument to a perfect night of love and friendship that was never to be forgotten Alfred was sobbing as he hugged Hagi while he wiped his nose on his hand.

Hagi was wearing huge white cotton Punjabi pants that night that were twisted tightly around his legs under a long starched white tunic. His enormous beard and all the hair on his head was free flowing in the moonlight over his gigantic belly so that his hair looked like a glowing halo of pale fuzz above a huge white mountain, this emotional Sikh, fragrant with the sweet scent of incense that he was forever burning in our powder room.

To say that Alfred loved Hagi Lamont Singh was an understatement. Alfred adored him, like he adored a lot of his friends that were slimes, I'm thinking. In fact Alfred loved a whole bunch of vile scumballs that anyone in his right mind would run away from like you'd run away from a rabid skunk, but not

Alfred. He loved some of the sleaziest dirtballs that anyone could ever imagine like for instance, Corbin Segal, who called himself a doctor, or that friend of his, Harold Hirsch, who's a compulsive gambler, who he trusted with his life, who would have sold Alfred down the river without batting an eye just to get his hands on thirty dollars.

Two days after we were all drinking and crying and singing in the orchard behind the house, Hagi Lamont Singh was hit by a cab as he was trying to get across Broadway at Thirty-fourth Street in New York City. Almost dead from wounds to his skull he rasped out to Alfred's partner, Carlo Pallivicini, an extremely tall Italian count who took enormous steps when he walked with his hands clasped firmly behind his back: "In dee . . . trosh . . . Masha . . . ott. . . . Meestah . . . Alfred Marvel's. . . ." That was as far as he got.

When we got the call, among the other details of Hagi's death, details that included a boil on his toe that was so infected that it made all the nurses want to vomit, a blood-sugar count that was over eight hundred, the pink silk nightgown trimmed in lace that he was wearing with a pink turban on his head in the hospital bed, Carlo Pallivicini whispered into the telephone that Hagi mentioned something about the trashmasher in our basement. In fact Carlo said, those were Hagi's last words, and since it was an unusual final thing to say, maybe it would be a good idea for Alfred to go down into the basement and take a look.

So up Alfred got, wiped his eyes, blew his nose, put on his six-hundred-dollar bathrobe that was piped in gold and his new black velvet bedroom slippers with gold crests on them and silently went down to the basement. Ten, fifteen, twenty minutes passed and no Alfred, so I got up, put on my fake bear-claw slippers and my old pink chenille bathrobe and went down after him to see what was going on.

There he was, pacing up and down with a big burlap bag in his arms that was maybe the size of a fifteen-pound bag of potatoes.

In stone silence we went upstairs as Alfred began to formulate a plan. First we'd throw our raincoats over our bathrobes. Then, in the kitchen like two zombies, we put the burlap sack into a big green trash bag that we had to try to seal several times with one of the little yellow wires that come in the box because our hands were shaking so badly. Then we ran out to the car and like two petrified rocks, in stone silence, we drove in the rain all the way to Captain Mac's Seafood Emporium at the inlet in Atlantic City which, at that time of year, was closed down for the season. Then while we were still in the car, we slit the garbage bag down the middle, put in the log we brought from our garage so that the bag would sink the instant it hit the water, then we opened the car door, made a dash across the west parking lot to the porch of the restaurant that extended out over the ocean and with one fling Alfred heaved the bag, turned, grabbed me by the arm and the two of us ran like streaks in our coats, bathrobes and bedroom slippers back across the porch, then through the west parking lot with the wet trees beside the road in that odd late-evening light making everything appear as if it had been draped in heavy copper satin. Then, as we sped off, we both started to hiccup out of nervousness.

It was September, the end of summer a year ago I'm thinking as I open my eyes and look at my watch and for a minute I feel a feeling of such immense desolation that it's hard to catch my breath.

Chapter

6

"Look!" I hear from over the row of books. "The jig's up. Okay! It's enough already! This big histrionic display, your genuflecting, etc., etc. I have my doubts about you," I hear.

And as I glance over there I see, yes, those same graying Brillo pads, the coal-black beady eyes and the astonishingly enormous beak are moving leftwards toward the end of the bookshelf while his eyes don't budge from my face for a second.

"Okay," he says, "so who are you anyhow and what are you doing sitting there like that, disturbing me for at least an hour and a half with all that sobbing and gasping or whatever it is you're doing. What's going on with you? That's what I'd like to know. Come on! Out with it! I've tried to shut you up at least ten times by now with sounds that any normal person would be sensitive enough to pick up instantly. But I see that simply isn't the way I'm going to get anywhere, is it?" he says as he steps out from behind the row of books.

He's a tall, rather handsome, dark, olive-complected man in a

Burberry trench coat, gray slacks, brown loafers, a gray tweed jacket under the open trench coat with a white oxford shirt and a dark striped silk necktie, all of it very high-grade looking, all of it expensive looking like maybe from New York or England or maybe even from the Riviera, and to top it all off he's holding in his hand a copy of *Robot Victory*—*the* masterpiece of the decade by my idol, Manuel Zot.

Some surprise! This is not your everyday weirdo, not by any stretch of the imagination, I'm thinking, as I stare at him. This is a very impressive-looking individual to say the very least and, moreover, he's holding a work of unblemished *genius!*

"Well?" he snaps as he glances at his black plastic wristwatch. "I don't have all day," he says in a bristly tone, not exactly rude but just a shade short of it.

"How would you like to join me for a cup of coffee," he says in an absolutely impersonal voice, "so you can tell me, if you know, why in the world you would sit on the floor, cry, take a deep breath, rotate your head, raise and lower your shoulders and then cry again. I don't get it," he says, as he gives out with a surprisingly wild, unexpected, bumpy, wholehearted laugh while he keeps peering at me with those steely beams like his eyes are the latest thing in high tech X-ray equipment. "Is this some kind of religious practice? Are you a Moonie or something?" he asks.

Hm-m-m-m, I'm thinking to myself, this fellow certainly appears to be on the normal side but of course who knows. After all, he *was* hiding behind a stack of books for well over an hour and a half and he *was* watching me the whole time and that's anything but normal. So the real question here is, Should I answer him and if so, what should I say because this kind of thing is extremely hard for me, this burden of conversation which I'm not good at, small talk, and besides that I can't forget what Alfred used to tell me.

"It's your *job!*" he'd say. "Women are supposed to be charming *conversationalists.* Therefore I expect you to charm the pants off of everybody at The American Fur Traders Convention, *Okay Peachy,* do you *understand?*" he'd say, like charm was a spigot I could just turn on and off.

But small talk isn't the real issue I'm thinking; I have to first make sure this person isn't some kind of nut, because he could be well dressed and even well-to-do and still be one of those very eccentric lunatics from tons of money who are killers or God knows what, because money's no guarantee. Remember Horace Beam, I'm thinking, who came from a very fine Jewish family, rich and religious and all of that, which didn't stop him from chopping that poor little Stanley Greenville into shreds because Stanley Greenville, unfortunately, was the one who was making the grocery delivery to the Beams that day. They said the blood was so thick into the wood in the ceiling of the dining room that the Beam family couldn't get even a fraction of what that house was worth. . . .

I'm noticing that this person is no spring chicken either. Another old fart, that's all that looks at me anymore. All the old lechers, they never stop trying, do they? Pigs! A lousy antique who ought to be ashamed of himself, I'm thinking to myself, as I finally decide not to answer him so as not to give him any wrong ideas. After all, the police in Vineland always tell you never to make eye contact (as if we didn't know that *anyhow!*) with any questionable individuals because who knows, they could take the most innocent gesture to mean anything they want, including an invitation to have *sex* with them I'm reminding myself as I try to make my demeanor more haughty by smoothing my skirt as I cross my legs while he's standing there scowling.

And as I'm looking and noticing the little lines between his eyes that look like a very short set of railroad tracks, for just that flash it registers that this person is really trying to be nice in spite of his strange and arrogant attitude. He probably has genuine goodwill toward me, and with that flash of understanding my tear spigot instantly turns on. Then comes the choking back of tears again with the quivering lower lip, and my eyes beginning to water while my nose is beginning to get all clogged up because *someone—anyone—is showing me a little kindness.*

"You see," I begin falteringly, but as I do I hear Alfred reminding me about how Jewish women always give too much instant information about themselves and about their deepest feelings, "Their hysterical *need!*" as he put it, "for *intimacy!* Why don't they just SHUT UP and PLAY TENNIS like the shiksas do instead of instantly telling anybody they run into on the street what makes them *tick!* Who *cares* what makes them *tick!*" he used to blast me. So I shut up.

"Look," he says, as he starts flashing his copy of *Robot Victory* at me, his finger in the middle to show me that he was supposedly reading behind the bookshelf.

Ha, I'm thinking, despite the fact that light doesn't even *exist* back there, and despite the fact that he didn't take his eyes off of me for even a fraction of a second the whole time he was back there—at least this book trick is with a decent book.

However, he's not fooling me, it's the oldest ploy in the world, this clown is just trying to impress me with his supposedly high-class taste in literature. *But fat chance,* old-timer! Even though I'm just a hick from Vineland, I wasn't born yesterday and furthermore I used to do that very thing with Karl Marx in Rittenhouse Square when I was maybe *seventeen* years old with the *Communist Manifesto* opened on my lap I'm thinking as he tips the book to his forehead in a fake-gracious half salute. "I can see that I should introduce myself before you decide if you want to have a cup of coffee with me," he says as he peers at me with those eyes that look like two steel bullets. "My name," he says as he makes a deep bow so that the book goes all the way up across his chest, "is Manuel Zot."

"Behind every fortune there's a crime."—*Alfred Marvel*

Chapter

7

Of course! I gulp, stunned by how stupid I am as I'm straining in the dim light of the bookstore trying to focus on him, my eyes pulling forward almost out of their sockets in an effort to grab hold of this man as if my eyes were claws. *Dummkopf!* I admonish myself under my breath, where is your *head!* Sure! *Of course!* That beak! Those eyes! Those fat graying Brillo pads springing out from above his ears! Only yesterday I read in the book section of the *Vineland Ledger* that this genius of all geniuses is in residence up at Harvard University this semester, so *certainly!* It was a whole front-page review of *Robot Victory* with naturally a stunning picture of him in a dark turtleneck leaning on his typewriter with all his novels, thirty-two of them if I'm not mistaken, in the bookcase behind him. I'm thinking as my eyes are glaring at him like my eyes are two strange nautical creatures that you sometimes see on Channel 39 that grow to be ten times their size when they're in danger. My wildest dream has come *true*

I'm thinking as I'm glaring at this man, dumbstruck with awe—So why does it feel more like a nightmare? The thing is, I need a little time to digest what's happening to me. I need to mull all this over a little so I can act in an appropriate manner. I need a hedge of some sort so I can stall him a minute while I gather myself. Life sure doesn't give you any warning, I'm thinking as I try without any luck to swallow. So what'll I do? Because naturally I don't know what to do under this kind of circumstance. Should I maybe try to say something or should I stay on the safe side and just keep quiet like I always do because who knows maybe my mother's right, maybe women should just keep their big mouths shut in general. And anyhow, what do you say to your *idol?* Tell me *that!* And yet, not to speak, to let this opportunity go would be the worst defeat of my entire life. Only, be honest, Peachy, what on earth could I possibly talk about to someone like *Manuel Zot?* Come *on!*

But wait a minute. Who on the face of this earth could ever possibly chat off the cuff, just like that, with *Manuel Zot?* Let's be fair, it occurs to me as I wipe the perspiration off my forehead. Even if he wasn't my most personally revered writer in the entire universe along with Saul Bellow, of course, Samuel Beckett, Celine and Philip Roth, I laugh to myself, so come on! Sure, maybe Einstein could joke around with Manuel Zot or maybe Dean Bok of Harvard University or Hannah Arendt *but who am I?*

As I smooth my skirt and try to fix my hair and then shoot another glance at this mountain in a Burberry trench coat who's towering in front of me, I notice he's glancing at his black plastic wristwatch. *God!* this *genius!* this Mount Zion or maybe Mount Olympus, take your pick, I'm thinking, this Manuel Zot is much more than just someone who eats and makes poo and snores and takes leaks and farts. Things like that belong to everyday people like Alfred and me and my father old Leo Fish but *not to Manuel Zot!* Are you *crazy.* People who write thirty-two novels before the age of fifty and *such novels!* these people are of a different ilk I remind myself as I'm digging around in my bag for my peppermints in case, God forbid, I've sprung a little halitosis.

"Well," he snaps, his eyes fixed on me again like two glaring suction cups, "would you, yes or no, *like to have a cup of coffee with me?* I only have forty minutes before I teach those little jerkoff artists a thing or two."

He has long spider fingers, flat pink seashell nails, extremely hairy fingertops and wrists, and because of a certain dark sharpness to his face that gives it a shadowy quality, he looks like a cross between Franz Kafka and a wild coyote.

"Yes, thank you very much." I manage to whisper, "I would love to."

And then to my own very great astonishment, I add, "Mr. Zot, I've just finished reading *Robot Victory,*" I mumble fast, "and it just so happens that I happen to have a copy of it here in my pocketbook so if I could bother you just a little more than I've already bothered you by my barging in on you like I have, which I assure you I'm very sorry about but anyhow, could I ask you," I whisper, "would it be too much trouble," I say, "to ask you to please autograph my book for me?" I manage to squeeze out of my mouth and lungs as I begin scrambling to get up to my feet, my heart pounding so hard my ears close up.

"Hold on," he snaps, his eyes lighting up. "Tell me," he says, "what do you carry around in that pocketbook beside your favorite novels?"

"Oh, not much." I laugh in a sickly way as I'm finally standing straight up in front of him, and standing to my surprise so close to him that it's hard not to touch him by accident.

"Come on," he laughs. "Let's see what else you've got in there."

"Nothing," I gasp as I clutch my bag to my body. "I tell you *nothing!"* I whisper as I begin to tremble from the sheer excitement of being this close to a world-famous writer who is also maybe the handsomest man I've ever laid eyes on in my entire life.

"Now come on," he says. "Let's not be coy," he says, as he blocks me so that I can't get past him while his hairy fingers suddenly dive into my bag like one of those seabirds you see on Channel 39 swooping down beak first from an enormous height for a little bit of fish. Then his hairy pincers surface a split second later with my can of Imported Israeli Gefilte Fish.

"Wait a minute!" He starts laughing uproariously. "Why, may I ask, does a woman carry *gefilte fish around in her pocketbook?* Do you have some kind of eating disorder to complement this religious fanaticism you practice on the floors of bookstores?

"What else do you have in there," he asks as his hairy seabird fingers dive in again and come up this time with the white cotton T-shirt I brought along in case I needed something cool to change into while I was driving.

"And what else?!" he asks as his fingers swoop down again.

"Stop, Mr. Zot, *please!*" I whisper, my knees buckling as I notice wildly, playful delight flying over his dark coyote face.

"Ah, let's see, yes, a green tennis ball," he laughs. "So, you play tennis beside being a Moonie with an eating disorder, huh? Very interesting." The hairy fingers swoop down again,

"And this, what's this?" He laughs as he comes up this time with a pair of panty hose. *"Ah ha!"* Dirty underwear. "I see," he says. "So you're a dirty little slut are you? Very interesting. Fascinating I might go so far as to say," he says as the fiendish fingers dive in again to come up this time with my copy of *Robot Victory.*

"Ah," he says, "so you read fancy literature, do you? Well, that makes you a jock religious fanatic with an eating disorder who is also a dirty little slut who likes to read good books. I see," he says. "So you read it, did you?" he laughs. "And you even *finished* it?" he says as he begins fiddling in his inside breast pocket for his pen. "Well, you deserve a fine reward," he says as he pulls off the top of the black felt-tip Flair with his teeth, tucks his own copy of *Robot Victory* under his arm and then turns to the wall. "What's your name?" he asks as he begins putting the date on the inside cover page in that funny, crabbed, turned-in way that left-handed people write.

"Peachy Marvel," I whisper, mortified to my marrow at having to divulge something as humiliating as my *name!*

"What?" he says.

"*Peachy Marvel,*" I whisper louder, sick at having to divulge something this unbearably revealing and humiliating twice! *To be nameless!* To remain without a *name* is to be *free!* Now I'm stuck! Now it's all different between us. Some mysterious thing has been shattered and now I'm under his scrutiny. Admit it, Manuel, I'm thinking, now you're getting hints about me because a name tells *everything!* Names are enormous give-aways, so of course you're making judgments about me, which is making my heart pound even harder if such a thing is even possible as he's scribbling away as indifferently as the sea.

"So," he says as he turns and hands me back my book, "what did you think of it?"

"Ah, you really did it this time," I manage to eke out to him, sick at my very soul at the very thought of what's coming next.

"Did *what?* What do you mean—*did it this time?*" he snaps.

"Oh well," I smile. "You know," I say, praying to God for enough time to collect myself and then maybe get a brainstorm.

"No, I don't know what you mean—'Did it this time.' What did I 'Do this time'? Surely you can be more explicit," he snaps at me again as cold as ice.

"Heh," I fumph as we begin walking toward the front of Wordsworth's Discount Bookstore, his eyes back on me again like the former high-tech X-ray beams I remember from behind the bookcase. "Well," I say, my tongue beginning to thicken. Come on, I'm thinking, don't let this happen, no attacks *please Peachy,* remember to "*just remember yourself*" like Ouspensky says in *The Fourth Way.*

Concentrate on your essence, Peachy, and then everything will work our perfectly, I'm thinking. Do you understand? Because *this can't kill you*, remember that. So if you just start saying anything that comes into your head while at the same time you concentrate on your essence everything will be *fine!* I'm coaching myself as I take a deep breath, look him in the eyes and then say, "Well, in my opinion, Mr. Zot, the book is a love letter to Calvin's mother and sister who were killed at the Robot's command." And my heart begins pounding so hard while we're walking that it feels like it's going to explode. Who am I and what am I even doing here and furthermore where did that sentence come from—how dare I spout off to the likes of *Manuel Zot* what I think of his *masterpiece*. Shut up Peachy, I think as I try again to swallow without any luck.

"Go on please," he whispers, "please continue."

"Well, like I said, Mr. Zot, *Robot Victory* is the masterpiece of a moment caught. Or maybe even less. Maybe it's just that fleeting feeling that we all have known from time to time, the fear, the rage that you've been able to grab hold of and run with, which is why I told my sister-in-law Loretta right after I finished it the other night, and why I just said to you a few minutes ago that you really *did it this time!* You were able to show the dream against the realness of the world, man's highest expression of decency against the most base natures in human existence and all in such an easy, everyday way, which is what's so amazing, not to mention of course the language you use, plain, nothing fancy, all in five-and ten-cent words."

"Precisely!" he says. "Better than classical music in my opinion because you see, language begins in the street but very soon it becomes the palace where our souls reside," he whispers.

"But they're making chopped liver out of me. What did you say you name is?" he says as he holds open the door for me to walk out of Wordsworth's and back onto Brattle Street.

"'Zot's thirst for blood'," he mutters, as we begin to walk. "'Zot's endless adoration of the mechanical person! Demented Manuel Zot, indeed disturbed, possibly even dangerous, hiding out at Harvard University,'" he seethes, as our pace picks up to almost a racing walk.

"*Time* Magazine ran a feature article on 'The bloodless, brutal world of Manuel Zot's mechanical order,'" he says as we're flying along. The man's obviously a jogger I'm thinking. "And a review in the *New Yorker* by none other than P. Harrison Torp says, 'Zot's inhuman experience and his defeat of all hope, corrupts, by its very existence, the human heart.'"

"What's that supposed to mean?" I pant as I dash along next to him as I'm gasping for air. "I don't understand what 'corrupts the human heart' means. If it means hopelessness, that's pure nonsense!" I gasp. "Evil corrupts the human heart and I ought to know," I say as I'm walking as fast as I can and as I'm blabbing, at the same instant exactly, I'm wondering why I said that! What do I know about evil, I'm wondering? *Who am I!* Where do I come off discussing *Robot Victory* or for that matter P. Harrison Torp of the *New Yorker* with this flaming genius whose face, *this face I'm running beside,* was just last week on *the cover of Time Magazine?*

"It seems to me," I say, "that people like P. Harrison Torp of the *New Yorker* write a lot of double-talk, Mr. Zot, and as far as I'm concerned," I gasp, "as long as it *sounds* good they're happy." I snicker. "All those rotten critics are born with a red pencil in their hands," I'm puffing as we're dashing around a corner. "You caught a whole chunk of life right at the spot where we are all pinned and squirming and lucky for mankind that you *did!*" I say. "You threw open the window of a secret room so that light could come in and flood the human *soul! Mr.* Zot."

"Tell me," he whispers as he grabs my elbow as we're dashing, "what did you think of Calvin Crut?"

"Oh *God,* Mr. Zot!" I gasp, as I'm trying to keep up with him. "Calvin Crut! His pain! He's like a turtle without a shell. Calvin Crut with his sore foot is a picture of how helpless all of us really are, and yet," I say, "instead of this embittering him, he turns his agony, like you did, Mr. Zot, into *art!* Calvin Crut didn't turn his rage against anyone, including himself," I'm gasping as I'm running along next to him. "Oh, no," I'm gasping, "instead he invented the Blood Machine! Out of torture beyond belief came something that wasn't there before. Instead of taking away from the world by a potshot at say the president of Lunatelles or maybe blowing up a rocket ship with thousands of people aboard which he had every reason to at least consider doing, what with what he had been through, oh no," I say, "instead, Calvin Crut invented something to *help* his fellow man. He turned his loss and rage into *art* just like you did, Mr. Zot, by inventing Calvin Crut out of your own rage and out of the depths of your own abject indignation. I read Nela Atwater's exquisite biography of you last year so I do know a little about you," I say, "if you'll excuse me for saying so. I mean about your mother being murdered when you were ten."

"What about Calvin's father?" he asks as he holds open the door of The Mug and Muffin Shop.

"Archie?" I say. "Archie Crut is an Old World being, a father in the whole sense of the word, not like nowadays when they take off at the drop of a hat or else they drive around with a bumper sticker that reads I'M SPENDING MY CHILDREN'S IN-HERITANCE. Archie's a lesson in sacrifice, honor and scruples. He stands for something! Tell me, Mr. Zot, where is there a place where any of us can find that kind of decency anymore *except* in art? It's a very sad commentary, granted, but nonetheless, Archie's someone who's worth living for and even worth dying for in an age when these very things are so hideously confused," I say as I slither into the booth across from Manuel Zot, who is sitting rock-like and intense across from me. Please, Peachy, I beg myself, shut up already—*okay?*

"Exactly," he whispers. "Archie *must* take sides because he knows that neutrality only helps the voice of *evil*. Oh, make no mistake," Zot smiles, "I know what a great accomplishment this book is. I know it's a tank loaded with heavy artillery and there's no one at the helm but *me*. Let me tell you, it rolls with 'Muscle and Beauty,' to quote Flaubert, and in that indeed it fulfills the requirement of fiction which is to observe and report. But I have gone one step farther. I have made *Art!* which is my knack," he says.

"For instance, when Archie sees the first robot coming into his luncheonette in Brooklyn and he drops his rag on the floor, gulps, and says, 'Okay fellows, what'll it be? Ham on rye or maybe you guys would like salami and scrambled eggs on wheat today?' I love that line," he says, as he starts laughing again in that surprisingly big, loud, bumpy, wholehearted way. "I love when Archie says, 'Okay fellows, what'll it be, Tab, Coke or Sprite?' And then Calvin says, 'Hey Dad, they don't want anything to drink. Okay, Dad?' Calvin says." And Zot laughs again.

"I'll tell you a little secret," Zot whispers as he leans forward over his menu. "The critics didn't get it," he says. "But then they never do because they don't know *dick!*" he whispers across the table. "All they have is their own stinking little subjective prejudices. In fact that's *who* they are! Lucky it isn't our lungs or our hearts they're chopping up.

"Am I right or am I right?" he looks at me. "I'll have you know that two thirds of all the books that are reviewed by those clowns are never even *read* by the person who's supposed to be reviewing it. They don't so much as even *glance* at it. Did you know," he says as he takes a sip of water, "that they have someone read it for them, report the gist and then they embellish, make judgments and crap around with it in their own words without knowing at all what the book is trying to even *address!*

"What would you like to eat?" he asks me as he opens the menu.

"Coffee," I say, "and a bran muffin, please."

"Coffee," he says to the waitress, "and a bran muffin for the lady.

"I will have a glass of orange juice but please, make sure there are no seeds or pith, dry toast, either rye or whole wheat, but please, no butter or cream cheese, a glass of skim milk, a cup of tea, but please, make sure there's no hot water in the saucer that might touch the tea bag, and please don't bring butter or cream cheese to the table because it nauseates me," he instructs the plump, uniformed executor of his fussiness.

"So," he says, turning back to me, "what did you say your name was?"

"Peachy," I answer him. "Peachy Marvel."

"What do you do besides cry on the floor in the back of bookstores?"

"You could say that I'm retired," I answer.

"Retired!" he says.

"Yes," I say. "Until this morning I was a full-time mother but I was relieved of that job today and before that I was a full-time wife, but I was relieved of that job, too, just about a year ago. So all in all," I smile, "I've just gone into retirement, which makes me cry on the floor in the back of bookstores," I say as my eyes well up and my lower lip begins to quiver as I begin fiddling with the paper napkin.

"How many kids?" he asks, as he starts wiping his fork with his paper napkin.

"One," I say, "who I've just deposited in Harvard Yard."

"What's his name?" he asks.

"Ruthie," I answer him.

"Do you have a picture?" he says.

"No," I tell him.

"Well, so where do you come from?" he asks.

"Vineland, New Jersey," I answer.

"Divorced, widowed, what?" he asks.

"My husband and I have been separated almost a year."

"*Hm-m-m-m,*" he says, his face lighting up. "Is it rough?" he asks.

"Very!" I answer.

"And I suppose you want him back," he says.

"If it were possible, which it isn't," I say.

"Why isn't it possible?" he asks as he starts laughing again in his big, bumpy, wholehearted way like my answer is maybe the funniest remark he's ever heard in his entire life.

"It's a long story," I say.

"What does that *mean?*" he asks.

"It means," I say as I look into his black beady eyes, "that I, Peachy Marvel, cannot undo certain things, as much as I wish I could."

"No one can undo anything," he says as he's watching his food being placed in front of him. "Maybe you're being a little overly dramatic," he laughs as he reaches into the inside breast pocket of his gray tweed jacket and pulls out first his black felt-tip Flair again and then a little blue spiral notebook. "Women are inclined to be that way, you know.

"What's your husband's name?" he asks as he begins jotting something down.

"Alfred," I tell him. "Why?"

"Because I'm fascinated with names," he answers as he's

writing a mile a minute in his crabbed, turned-in backwards, left-handed way.

So I'm thinking, by him, women are all overly dramatic; by Alfred, Jewish women demand intimacy at the drop of a hat, and according to my mother, "Women should just keep their big mouths shut on general principles," which all points to a big, worldwide underground club of women haters out there I'm thinking as I break my muffin in half.

Hm-m-m-m-m-m, so maybe Ruthie and her friends were really on to something. Maybe, *just maybe* they weren't *completely* crazy after all, I'm thinking as I take a bite.

"Are you Jewish, Italian, Greek or what?" he asks as he's writing.

"Jewish," I snap. "Why?"

"*Why?*" he says. "Because Jewish women are a whole category unto themselves," he laughs. "The hysteria! The terrors! The tits! The hair! The lips!" he's laughing as he's writing, his tongue tipping out from the corner of his mouth ever so slightly as he's scribbling away a mile a minute.

"So, Mr. Zot," I say, feeling a drop more confident as I take a sip of my coffee, "could I ask you for your opinion about something?" I say, thinking to myself that maybe now is the perfect moment to do a little fieldwork to find out if Ruthie and all her friends are in fact onto something or if wisdom, riches, and all the fruits of life still belong to the old hard-liners like me, my mother, Granny Heinfling and Manuel Zot.

"Be my guest," he says as he looks up.

"Well," I say, "not all of it, but a lot of the trouble began when my husband started seeing a psychiatrist. That's when I began to realize that guilt is the culprit that ruins marriages."

"No surprise," he says as he picks up his knife and fork. "On the one hand psychiatrists are often real evil-doers, make no mistake about that!" he says. "And on the other hand, guilt is always there, isn't it?

"What's the psychiatrist's name?" he asks as he puts down his fork, takes out his black felt-tip Flair again, and begins writing.

"Corbin Segal," I say as I take a bite of my muffin.

"Look, Mr. Zot," I say, "I hope what I'm about to discuss with you isn't going to one day appear in any of your books."

"No promises," he says as he's writing. "Remember, I'm a writer first and a human being second, which means in plain English that *nothing is sacred!* Those are the ground rules, okay? So now, tell me," he says, "what about this Corbin Segal?"

"Well, to begin with," I say, "he's a short, fat blimp with a huge potbelly so that he sort of looks like Humpty Dumpty with red cheeks, pointy ears and rimless mounting glasses and when he laughs he sounds like a hyena. But the most telling thing about him are his dead eyes that just stare out of their sockets at you like there's no one in there. Plus," I say, "he's an Advertising Psychiatrist, which means he comes on immediately after the eleven P.M. news on the weekends. There he is, sitting behind a big oak desk with an extremely compassionate look on his face as he's spouting all this garbage. You know: 'Are you anxious? Do you feel abandoned? Is depression ruining your marriage? Tell me,' he says, 'Is your life less than it could be under the circumstances of your limitations? Well,' he says as the camera comes in close, 'I can help you become the person you and your family would like to see you become. Discretion is my middle name,' he smiles as the information about where to call including an 800 number for out-of-town clients appears in a big white subtitle. 'And of course,' he says, as the ad fades away, 'credit cards are gladly accepted.'"

"No!" Manuel Zot starts laughing. "My *God!* He sounds like one of those late-night cable television cunts who gives phone jobs that you can put on your MasterCard.

"Hello," Zot says into a pretend telephone that he makes out of his soup spoon. "This is Dr. Corbin Segal and I've been waiting for your call. If you'll just give us your American Express card number or your Visa or your Diner's Club and the expiration date," he says, "we can get down to the business of making you into someone else. Do you want to be a person who can lie with a straight face? Do you want to be able to kill, rob or just fuck anyone and everyone on the face of the globe? *No problem!* All you have to do is go out and buy ten gallons of Hägen Daaz Rocky Road, recite the National Anthem backwards, count to thirty-five inside out and stand on your head for seventy-five seconds and I promise you'll never sit home alone on another New Year's Eve. Okay? Fine! Good night and Good morning," he shouts as he throws his head back all the way and lets out a whooping laugh that rocks the whole Mug and Muffin Shop.

"Tell me more about this Corbin Segal," he says as he picks up his fork and starts eating again.

"Well," I say, "practically every other minute he's a guest

speaker on Good Morning Vineland, which is a local radio program that interviews big shots from the whole New Jersey area, and on this program he tells everybody they have to live their lives like you squeeze an orange. The last drop of juice is your *moral responsibility* to extract for yourself because if you don't look out for Numero-Uno he says, you can bet your 'Sweet Bippy' no one else is going to."

"No!" Zot whispers, his eyes riveted to my face again, the food on his plate abandoned.

"Yes," I say. "Also," I say as I take a bite of my muffin, "he holds weekly seminars on greed," I say as I put some butter on the little piece I'm holding.

"On greed!" he whispers.

"That's right," I say.

"Alfred is no fool I can assure you," I say, "but let me tell you he took Dr. Segal very seriously. I mean, every word was Holy Writ. Like for instance, Dr. Segal believes you only do what makes you feel good or what's fun or what gives you a real 'kick'. That's what he calls 'healthy morality.' You're never supposed to consider the other person first, or, according to Dr. Segal, you're a moral martyr and all moral martyrs are extremely depressed whether they know it or not."

"Wait, don't go so fast," Zot mutters as he scrambles for his pen and notebook. "I can't write fast and you're going very fast, so please," he says, "let me catch up. Hold it a second, wait okay," he's muttering as he's zooming along backwards in that funny crabbed, turned-in left-handed way. "I think you said something about greed," he says. "What were you saying?"

68

"Oh, that," I say. "Every Monday night fifteen prominent New Jersey businessmen come to Dr. Segal's house to discuss various aspects of 'healthy greed,' as he calls it, because to squash greed according to Dr. Segal is to repress serious elements of self-preservation that should be cultivated.

"But I can't complain about all this," I say as I take another bite of my muffin, "because I was the one who sent my husband there in the first place."

"You *what?*" Zot whispers as he looks at me.

"That's right," I say as I take a sip of my coffee. "I was beginning to worry about the way that Alfred kept looking at me so I turned to Corbin Segal because I've known him since he was a boy, plus he was an old friend of my brother Charlie's. In fact, they went to medical school together."

"How was your husband looking at you?" Zot whispers as he whips out his pen and notebook again.

"Very judgmentally," I say.

"It started with him getting quieter and quieter. Then he began taking a lot of business trips so that he wasn't home for long periods at a time and when he did come home he began to question everything: What I did, where I went, who I went with and always it was as though he was really angry at me. I could feel the edge of his anger coming at me from every angle only he wouldn't come right out and tell me what he was angry at so I figured maybe he was in love with someone else," I say as I take another bite of my muffin. "I even considered putting a private detective on him, which, of course, was my mother's idea, but at the very last minute I backed off because I felt that even if he was in love with someone else it was my fault anyhow. I mean, if he was running around with women it was because I drove him to it because, you see, Alfred was never that kind of man."

"*Hm-m-m-m*," Zot says as he's writing again like there's no tomorrow.

"So that's when I went to see Corbin because I was so confused and crazy by then that my imagination had become my whole intelligence. But I went to him as a friend, not as a patient and the next thing I know the money-hungry slime has *Alfred* in therapy *six days a week* at two hundred dollars a clip. It's like paying a thousand dollars to have a shirt ironed or twenty dollars to mail a letter. And yet the more Alfred paid it seemed like the more he fell under the spell of that raucous evil megalomaniac, Dr. *Fraud!* The man was an alcoholic, he was a dwarf who weighed a ton, he has no friends, his wife left him for a woman and both his sons don't speak to him. This is the dirtball that sucked my husband in like he was a human vacuum cleaner.

"He and Alfred began taking walks in the woods, all day sometimes because he had no other patients, or else they would spend weekends in New York 'gallery hopping' because, to quote Corbin Segal, 'Art doesn't talk back!' Every other second there was another Corbinism coming out of Alfred's mouth until it was as if Alfred were the puppet of some gigantic invisible ventriloquist whom I couldn't my hands on or get out of my life.

"He started coming to all our parties and he was always the obnoxious center of all the attention. No one could ever get a word in edgewise once Corbin Segal started talking while his new girlfriend would sit there in a blue-white rage while she kept gazing at her wristwatch.

"Or else we were summoned to the Y every Tuesday night to hear him talk on *greed! Human vagaries! Sexual stamina,* I and II! *On art and the madman in our society,* and finally the incredibly stupid course he gave called 'Color Your World Hilarious.'

"And as if that wasn't bad enough, Corbin Segal finally went into business with Alfred."

"What was it? What kind of business?" Zot whispers, his high-tech X-ray eyes riveted to my face like I held the secret of the universe under my upper lip.

"The drive-in funeral business," I say, knowing I'm on a roll. I feel myself gaining confidence with each passing minute.

"The what?" Zot whispers incredulously.

"Please!" I say as I take a bite of my muffin. "It made Corbin Segal a millionaire within a year! The body was mounted on a revolving marble slab in the middle of a big fenced-in parking lot," I begin as I take a sip of my coffee. "The mourners arrive through an elegant gate. They drive up to the bereavement book that's set on something like a fast-food window. The mourner reaches out of his car window, signs the book, takes the white carnation out of the basket (or any flower for that matter that the family decides it wants), then the mourner drives up to the revolving slab where the coffin is, he throws the flower that he picked up at the bereavement window onto the box which may or may not be open, keeps going till he hits the back exit gate where he receives a wipette packet, a cup of coffee and two

pieces of *schnecken* and he's out of there just in time for a business meeting or a movie or anything else he might want to do that day because according to Dr. Segal this is what's known as 'healthy death.'

"This is the 'future' according to Corbin Segal, M.D., P.C. No chest beating! No angst! No wailing and no shiva either which, according to Dr. Segal, is outdated and extremely hostile to the family of the deceased. 'On With Life' is his motto. The victim was lucky to have had his sixty-some-odd years in the first place. 'After all,' says Dr. Corbin Segal, who by the way is obsessed with death himself, 'his birth was but a fluke, his death a certainty.' The real trouble with everything is *expectations!* REMEMBER—NO ONE LIVES FOREVER is written in gigantic script above the entrance gate as you drive in and LET THE GOOD TIMES ROLL is written in the same enormous black lettering as you drive out the exit gate, because *The lesson of death, according to Corbin Segal, is reality!* Not sentimentality and not guilt!" I say as I take another bite of my muffin while I'm thinking shut up Peachy, you're talking too much.

"Look," Zot says, "I have a class in less than four minutes but I'll be free after that for the rest of the day and all night. Stick around," he says. "Have another cup of coffee while you're waiting. Read a couple chapters of *Robot Victory* and I'll be back in forty-five minutes on the dot."

And with that *The Manuel Zot* glances at his black plastic wristwatch, grabs his trench coat, slithers out of the booth and dashes off.

"Woulda coulda shoulda."—*Granny Heinfling*

Chapter

8

*I*f I were only ten years younger I'm thinking as I watch Manuel Zot slip into his trench coat, push open the door of The Mug and Muffin Shop and then vanish back out into the world he came from—Cambridge—with its five-story bookstores, coffeehouses, dark grained window casings and rambling overgrown lawns that all echo a tradition of civilized intellectual life.

So who am I? I'm thinking, intimidated by the world I find myself presently sitting in as if I were the poorest relative at the ball. He said to "stick around." But I'm thinking, *that* was a neat trick to make his getaway easier because let's face it, escape is always a tricky business. And anyhow I'm thinking, as I take a sip of my coffee, why would a man like Manuel Zot ever in ten billion years *ever look at me?*

Maybe ten years ago, but today, *come on!* I'm forty-five years old and no eye-catcher anymore. And what's more, even my history is very unremarkable. I grew up across the highway from my grandfather's chicken coops in Vineland New Jersey. I was

married when I was barely eighteen years old and I never saw
the inside of a college dorm until yesterday when I unpacked
my daughter's trunk in her fourth-floor room at Stoughton Hall.
Our only fame had been the fact that my grandfather's chicken
coops were the biggest money producers in all of Cumberland
County. In fact, that was my family's whole claim to fame for as
far back as I can remember. You might say chickens and eggs
were our family's whole past glory, I'm thinking, as I pat up the
remaining crumbs from my muffin and then lick them off my
finger. And boy! Manuel Zot would have really been impressed
by that, wouldn't he? Like he'd really be impressed with the
information that my grandfather didn't even have land to speak
of either, not in comparison to the corn and tomato farmers or to
the big peach growers who flanked him on either side. Even the
little sweet potato farmers had more ground than my grandfather's run-down coops that looked like they'd blow over if
somebody even sneezed on them. But let's face it Peachy, that's
what I know and that's who I am, the hayseed descendant of a
stiff little chicken farmer who had immensely thick eyeglasses
and a rim of bright orange hair that his wife used to henna for
him while he sat in front of the coops snapping the necks of the
sick chicks so fast it was hard to believe that life, at least as far as
chickens were concerned, had any meaning. Money, yes! but
life? That was a different story. No fancy feed for his stock, I'm
thinking as I take another sip of coffee, no siree! Grandfather
Heinfling sure knew how to keep prices at rock bottom till the
instant he sold them to the Campbell Soup Company which

was practically the same day their laying time was done. In and out, one, two, three. Eggs—Soup!

"Who needs air and space for those stinking miserable cannibals," he'd yell with that fat cigar he was always chomping on plugged in his mouth like it was some kind of permanent facial attachment.

"Why, they'd peck their own children to death if they had half a chance," he'd yell with such vehemence you could feel a whole lifetime of chicken hatred searing out of every pore in his wiry old body.

But the fact is they *are* cannibals I'm thinking, which was why they had to be debeaked practically the minute they were hatched by a hideous machine that *zap*—snipped off half their faces with a flaming little guillotine knife because otherwise, God!—one scratch from a piece of chicken wire or from a nail or from God knows what and the poor stinking devil who got cut and shed even one drop of blood would be eaten by the others in less than a minute flat, which was why my grandfather had to have a red bulb burning in there twenty-four hours a day in order to distract them.

I could tell Manuel Zot a lot about the way chicken coops smell, I'm thinking. He'd love to hear about that, I'm sure. Or I could tell him about the license plate attached to a stick by the back porch steps so Grandmother Heinfling who worked in there all day could scrape the shit off her shoes before she went inside the house. Or maybe I should tell him about my grandfather's position on good and evil: "The chickens that eat the wounded in two seconds flat aren't *bad* because in nature there is no such thing as bad—only survival," he'd laugh as he chomped on his cigar.

Or maybe I could tell Manuel Zot how my brother Charlie and I used to have to walk two and a half miles to the school bus stop and two and a half miles back every day, rain or shine. Snow, freezing wind, it didn't matter, all that mattered was to be in the house by night because nights in Vineland, I could tell him, had the kind of darkness that to this day if I look straight ahead into just the thickness of it I still feel like I'm expanding. I could tell him I still feel like I'm puffing up bigger and bigger and bigger until finally I feel like I'm some kind of gigantic blob that just keeps on expanding and swelling and puffing in order to fill the big dark void that's all around me everywhere. I would try to seek its limits with a toe or with a finger and then I could tell him how I used to have to grab my brother Charlie's arm to anchor myself in all that pitch dark blackness. And I could also tell him how I'd look straight up at those zillion blazing lights, those dazzling wild worlds up there like the Little Dipper or the Great Boreal Zenith, which I could find in one glance in mid-sky and then, *zap*—I was a speck, a grain or the smallest, most inconsequential ant that ever crawled the earth without a shadow.

The peach orchards directly across from my grandfather's coops had the best Elberta Freestones on earth. Each one of the Humbert peaches was like a perfect little globe of the world. Just the sheer beauty of those washed out yellows that blended into the palest pink as it swirled up toward a stem that was sunk into a green and white indentation was astonishing and they were huge! Maybe half a pound each with warm fuzzy skin that felt almost human.

But there was a big difference between the Humberts who had owned that tract for over a hundred and thirty-five years and all the rest of the growers in the area, a distance the Humbert family never let anybody forget, and distance is power. That's why, probably out of nothing but pure spite, Alfred and I used to sneak into those orchards late at night when we were certain no one was around and with Alfred on the lookout I'd quick whip off my bandanna and then gather into it as many of those exquisite little masterpieces as I could get and not so much because we even wanted to eat them either, I'm thinking as my eyes well up. We started doing that when I was pregnant with Ruthie because from about the fifth month on the urge to steal was so overwhelming that if I wasn't stealing peaches, then it was thoughts of robbing banks or snatching purses that were sometimes so strong I'd be afraid to go out on Landis Avenue alone I'm thinking as the waitress pours more coffee into my brown stoneware mug.

"So Peachy!" Alfred used to say when he was bored, "Were you always faithful? *Ah,* come on, tell me the truth. Come on," he'd say. So I used to laugh. That's how I'd answer him I'm remembering as I pour in the cream and begin to stir. Who would even want me? I'd laugh but the fact was, I was always aware of the way they watched me, the eyes of all those men on the dance floor or out on the pier where we went fishing, the way the dock hands would look at me down where we kept the boat that was tied to its moorings with all those ropes and when I'd see them looking I used to get secretly afraid that maybe I had somehow missed it all, afraid I had missed something that flowed away from me over all those afternoons of always being faithful to him, so that I missed some other man, the *real* man, some big, dark, tall man whom I was always afraid I'd miss somehow, and then I'd end up like my mother, a piece of fine glazed china bric-a-brac on a shelf somewhere and feel like she does now, all alone and lonely, like the whole thing got to be for her. So I tried not to think at all with owning a lot of doodads and making a lot of endless vows about never looking at any-body as long as I lived and things like that. Only I was the child, no matter what I felt or vowed, who ran to greet him every night at five with my braids still flying in the wind behind me as I ran and always in my eyes the secret picture of that dark big man I was always so afraid I'd never find in some ratty old tweed jacket who had his arms around my dolls and his monogram on all my sheets and towels. Okay, so maybe it wasn't you after all, Alfred, whom I was faithful to, maybe it was to some dream I had or to some longing down by those fields that Christmas when I wasn't even eighteen yet and I buried his silver comb beside the dog who used to run with me.

Too neat for my two cents, the way Hendella had to have the dishes stacked in piles always with those orange paper napkins in between and all her little porcelain ballerinas and all her little china snails and the little china flowers in their little china flower pots on every shelf in the sun room. Everything in its place and a place for everything was her motto all right, as she put the butter on her roll or took another bite of meat and then siphoned off two carrots with no expression on her face. While me, *ha!* All my clothes were always all over the bed just so I could find the right one and all my shoes with all the tissue paper, and the empty boxes everywhere with my bureau drawers opened at all different levels so that it was always like some huge jumble of colors tumbling out everywhere, with the closet doors thrown wide open in order to eye all those damn little lined-up soldiers in there who stood headless and legless next to scarlet tulles and midnight velvet and a gray lace skirt thrown across the back of the chair looking dead for having let the lady down, until finally the whole place was one big mess in some other form and then again in some new other form again. Riding down the street—gorgeous day—the men digging by the side of the road stop and shout so I shout back, zipping through the Acme the men who weighed the vegetables would always stop and turn and I'd look back, and then prancing into the bar at the club and watching the men all come smiling over like well-dressed sewer rats including all his friends, too, while I'd look in the mirror above the rows of whiskey bottles to fix my hair and catch a glimpse of my face all puffy then with how young it was. And how every head would turn as we walked out of there. And, oh God, how Alfred loved it. It drove him so crazy the way men noticed my satin dress and my black lace stockings and that black wool suit we bought in Amsterdam and those terrific Italian shoes and all that Jungle Gardenia perfume I used to wear and how Alfred would stop dead in his tracks and sure there were always other women and pretty ones too but he never saw a soul, all he'd do was stare at me not even blinking like he was in some kind of trance or something he was so mad about me then, and although he'd never say a single word I could tell that he was dumb with admiration especially when those men at the club in their tuxedos were all standing at the bottom of the stairs and they all turned to stare at me with my hair up real high. The night I wore that pink wool gown when my hair was long and over to the left a little with all those pink tea roses stuck in there and God he loved it, I had it all done up that way to make the blackness even blacker. The way he beamed when his best customer at the fur traders' convention came over to buy us a drink and he just stood there so wild with happiness he couldn't wait till he got me home and though he never knew exactly what it was about me, because I certainly wasn't all that pretty or anything, but he loved me more that night than anyone had ever loved me in my life I'm thinking as I look down into my coffee mug, twenty-six years ago, I'm thinking as I gaze at the tattered waitress with her pockmarked face and dyed blond hair.

Before all these stinking little heartless lines, these crow's feet as they're called, had begun to groove in all around my eyes and my hair, *phew! Please!* I'm thinking, but Manuel Zot did say "stick around."

Manuel Zot, Peachy! You've spent the whole morning with maybe the most famous and brilliant writer in the *world* who, let's not forget, was spying on you for quite a while before *he* started talking to *you!* That's right! The man who was spying on you, Peachy, just so happened to be *the Manuel Zot who wrote Robot Victory* and that's not chopped liver—right? I'm smiling to myself as I nip off a tiny piece from the crusty ridge of the top of my new corn muffin which makes me think of the corona of a man's business. But who would even believe it? Would Alfred? Would Ruthie? Would your mother? Not in a million *years,* which all goes to show you that life is much wilder than fiction, I'm sneering. Who could ever even invent such a thing as this? Fiction's *nothing* compared to the way it really happens in this life, which is why fiction's such a stinking bore! All that trumped *down* storytelling, *garbage* with a beginning, a middle and an end when there isn't any, so it's all pornography in books—lies! junk! that's all it is! Untruth for the most part, pure fabrication with none of the irony which is the whole secret, I'm thinking as I take a sip of coffee. But *not science fiction,* Manuel! Now that's imagining, that's *inventing* with a capital "I." That's *visionary* with a real sense of society woven into the basic imagination of the plot so that the whole picture is *grand, elegant* and *elaborate,* which translated, means, *That's writing!* I'm thinking as I picture myself introducing Manuel Zot to Alfred at my niece Suzie Fish's wedding, which is to take place in less than two weeks. Alfred, I'd say, I'd like you to meet my good friend Manuel Zot. I smile as I take a bite of my new corn muffin, and as I do the first real grin I've had in months comes over my face like some gigantic Cheshire cat that's gone completely off its rocker.

It would also be a pleasure, I'm thinking, to show my mother,

Madam Hendella Fish, a thing or two I smile again as I take another bite. She with her secret contempt for me because Alfred is gone—right? Because she would have stuck to old Leo Fish no matter what she felt, the same as Granny Heinfling would have held onto old Sam the Chicken Man no matter what, but not me, Hendella—not me, Granny Heinfling. I'm from the *Let's get divorced generation*—right? This generation—*my* generation is getting divorced all over the place because if we didn't we'd be *dead* from the silences, Hendella! *Dead,* Granny Heinfling from what was never said but felt, Understand? You dried-up old prune, I'm thinking who doesn't weigh more than forty pounds with your flounce of soft blue birdy hair and that schnoz of yours that's worse than the beak on any chicken you ever slipped an egg away from, you should have been debeaked yourself, you who's been snarling at me from over your grapefruit sections from the day that Alfred walked out the door! you tough old turkey wing who knows everything under the sun, you oracle with your bony elbows. So who's Manuel Zot? you're asking. Only a world-famous writer and only the visiting professor of literature at Harvard University this semester, you lousy little dried-up toothpick. And that goes for you, too, my beloved brother Charlie Fish with that schnoz of yours that's exactly like the little old bat's.

How could you and your lousy wife Loretta Finkel have *ever in ten million years invited Alfred Marvel to Suzie Fish's wedding?*
Tell me that!
Where was any loyalty to me!
Could I have *ever* in ten million years done a thing like that to

you? And I take a sip of water to steady myself against the onslaught that begins boiling up at them all over again.

Well, I whisper to the brother and to the sister-in-law whom I had once considered the closest friends I had on the face of the *earth,* if Alfred Marvel comes to Suzie Fish's wedding, *count me out!*

"Once a man really falls in love, he never falls out."
—*Alfred Marvel*

Chapter

9

*I*t's been a long time since I've seen Alfred I'm thinking as I glance at my watch and then take a sip of coffee.

It's almost a year since I've seen the way his neck jerks when he's nervous and his red flaming ears and his eyes that have looked at me since the day that Nancy was killed like I'm a monster. Not that he ever came right out and said anything to my face, but it didn't take much for me to know what he was thinking. Every time he looked at me he was thinking that I could have done better and maybe he was right.

The day it happened he was sore at me from the minute he opened his eyes, maybe because business was bad, or because he had a fight with the bank, or maybe his sister was hitting him on the head with a lot of bills because he was the one who took care of her and all her kids because that was the way their father left it in the will. So when I stopped by his office that afternoon, and brought up the subject of a new car he really hit the roof.

"One day it's one thing, the next day it's something else," he started. "One week it's a new fur coat, the next week it's a grandfather clock but not just any grandfather clock, oh no," he said, "not for Patricia Marvel! For Patricia Marvel it has to be a priceless *treasure* that has papers from Lehmann Brothers in Bucks County. So okay, sure, fine with me. *And* the new fur coat *and* the Nagucci coffee table. Everything Peachy wants Peachy gets. So the next thing was a farm in Downingtown, okay, fine! But then, no, she changes her mind. Instead she wants a place at the beach. But not in Nantucket or in Martha's Vineyard which would be okay with me," he said, "because that way I could get a little sailing in. No, she has to have a house in Loveladies Harbor New Jersey where all those Philadelphia dingbats go. But again, fine! If that'll make her happy we'll sell the farm in Downingtown before we close on it. But wait a minute, no, she says she doesn't want the beach house, instead now it has to be a house on the rocky coast of *Maine* which to me," he says, "is like going straight to *jail! Why Maine? What's* going *on!*" he started yelling at me like he had been yelling at me the day before because when he came home from the office and saw four boxes of Andrew Geller shoes on the table in the hall you'd think the world was coming to an end.

"What are you trying to do," he yelled. "Up in your closet there are at least eighty pairs of shoes, *Peachy.* You only have two feet. But no," he was shouting, "she has to have every pair of shoes that were ever made and not only that, she has to try all of them on for me which drives me *crazy* because as far as I'm concerned they all *look exactly the same.* But okay! Fine! Anything she wants, okay? So then she wants to take piano lessons and I say fine! Great, maybe practicing will keep her out of the stores for maybe an hour or two."

He was glaring at me, so naturally when I had to ask him about the car he really hit the roof.

"A *what?*" he asked.

"A Checker Marathon," I said, as his neck began to jerk.

"*What for!*" he asked. "Damn it, Peachy," he said, "there's not a damn thing wrong with the car you've got!"

"Please Alfred," I whispered.

"Please *what!*" he snapped.

"The Checker Marathon," I said. "The Chevy station wagon handles like a *jet!* I can't park it," I told him, "every time I take it out I put a dent in it and although I can't exactly put my finger on what the problem is I tell you that every time I put my foot in that damn car I get so scared because the car doesn't handle right.

"*Something's wrong with it Alfred, so please!* Alfred, all you have to do is write out a check. *Okay? Listen to me.*

"*There's something wrong with that Chevy station wagon.*" I was pleading with him but since it was at his office and since everybody could hear everything he got *really* mad.

"*No more!*" he shouted. "*Just forget it, Peachy! Enough—Okay! Forget the Checker Marathon,*" he was raging at me. So I grabbed Nancy and ran out of there, jumped in the Chevy station wagon and tore off.

It was on a morning in May when everything was new yellow

just before the rush of green. Spring—the air was soft out the window of the car as I was flying down the road with the baby standing on the front seat next to me. I know Alfred thinks I should have had her fastened in the car seat but she was the kind of child who you couldn't keep still for more than a minute anyhow, so the second she'd get into that car seat she'd begin struggling and climbing to get out and since she had one of those redheaded tempers just like her father—it was always a battle between us. So sometimes when I felt particularly power-ful like nothing bad could ever happen to me and certainly never to her, I'd let her stand beside me on the front seat while I drove with one arm holding her across the stomach. Only that day a hot rod came in behind me up at the top of the hill maneuvering so fast and gunning his gears so close on my tail that I couldn't even see his headlights. Maybe I was going too fast which I'm sure to this day Alfred thinks I was. Certainly it wasn't more than forty but on those back roads maybe forty was like going ninety on the Garden State Parkway, and with that hot rod right on my tail I couldn't slow down when two big white poodles ran into the street at the bottom of the hill directly in my path.

The only thing I could possibly have done would have been to kill the dogs, but I couldn't think that fast. The instinct that says you don't kill even a squirrel was so drummed into me that all I could do was swerve the car to avoid hitting them as I slammed my foot down so hard on what I thought was the brakes. And that's when the blue Impala Station Wagon shot way off to the left and then flew ahead a million times faster, it seemed, than it had been going as a low stone wall, a thick green privet hedge, a broken fence and a tree were all suddenly racing toward us.

Then, in some strange, protracted sense of time it all got very still as if the baby and I were sailing over the clearest, smoothest water into a catastrophe I had expected all my life—a catastrophe like a woman at the top of the stairs I had kept waiting long enough.

She died with only one little sound like gulls make.

For a long time after that I heard that sound coming out of the electric coffeepot and out of the vacuum cleaner. It came out of the metal cart I pushed around the Quality-Plus Food Market up in Rosenhayn. It came out of my bread box and out of my car door and out of the gate at the back of the drive. I couldn't tell Alfred about it because I knew he would think that I deserved to hear it coming out of a million more things than that because I saved myself by hanging onto the steering wheel with both hands while I let her die. He never said a word but I could see in the way he looked at me that that's what he was thinking, so finally I couldn't stand to have to look at him anymore because I couldn't stand to see that look.

Not that it helped, but out on the road, with my left hand I tried to apply pressure to stop the bleeding by squeezing her neck together where it had been sliced while at the same time I pressed my right hand hard against her temple to try to stop the rest of the hemorrhaging, and all the time I was looking for my pocketbook because my credit cards were in it and a couple of checks that had already been endorsed.

As I walked out into the street with the baby upside down in my arms, her face with her eyes wide open pressed against my ribs, my feet sloshed in the puddles of blood that were in my shoes. My dress was so drenched in blood it stuck to my body like heavy, wet, sweet-smelling newspapers and my hands and legs were caked. A car passed I remember, but it didn't stop. It just kept going. Another car came over the hill and kept on going, and then, finally, a third one came and that one stopped. A man leaped out, jumped the privet hedge across the road and disappeared into a house on the other side of the street as a fourth car came, screeched to a stop, a boy who was in the front jumped in the back, and we got in. The driver was a jittery little man who looked like a pebble, balding, with gray hair, and he was blue and chubby in the face.

He wore a white open neck short-sleeved shirt that had little green kites on it. The boy in the back was no more than fifteen years old and as the man started driving the boy put his arms around my shoulder and started talking to me and rocking me as the man was speeding with his hand on the horn. The man drove up on the curb as he made a turn, he rammed the car in front of him at the first red light and then after that, with his hand jammed down on the horn the whole time he took the second light without even stopping and all the time his nonstop gibberish while the young boy in the back kept rocking me in his arms and talking to me till we got to the emergency entrance of Cumberland Memorial Hospital, where a bunch of people all in white were waiting for us outside in the sunshine.

There were no shadows anywhere. Nothing but the glare of

the sun on the clump of people who were all in white and one nurse coming towards me whom I handed the baby to—I didn't want to look at her anymore. Out of cowardliness I wanted to get as far away from the baby as I could get. I would have eaten her out on the road where it happened if I could have, like an animal, and been done with it that way, that's what I was thinking as black police cars came zigzagging into the parking lot like crows flying in on a little crumb of bread. . . .

Then someone led me through sliding automatic double doors and then into a sterile room that had a huge operating table with a gigantic light shining over it and that was when the clean, efficient horror of medicine started. As the fog of activity began swirling around me with strange smells, strange fingers touching me and the strange faces of all the nurses as they began taking off my dress and my bra and my underpants that were all five times their weight in blood. The blood was so hard by then that it was like one big crust that covered my legs and my hands and my feet, between my toes there were little solid sticks of blood and as the nurses were silently scrubbing at them they were smiling at me and what was really strange was that I was smiling back.

They smiled as they put the clamps to my forehead to stop the bleeding. They smiled as they helped me into a white hospital gown. They smiled as they helped me up onto the litter that was aimed for surgery and I smiled back as they kept smiling quietly. Then someone who had been yelling orders out in the hall, probably the administrator of the hospital, came in as I was lying on the litter and as he smiled at me I was thinking how this was a big day.

Oh boy, I was thinking, *ha!* Not just another little dog bite or split lip, no siree, this was not some little tetanus booster—this was the big time, this was a story to tell his wife and neighbors and all the guys at the bowling club for the next ten years I was thinking, as the smiles kept coming from everyone. And as I was smiling back I kept my eye on the door, expecting at any moment not Alfred or even the baby to come into the room, but Insanity!

What would it look like? I was wondering.

Probably it would be made of pewter or silver. Or maybe it would be made of diamond dust with black leather gloves. I figured it would turn me immediately into a piece of bright green tissue paper that would fly up and get caught in a tree where I would have to wait until the wind came up to take me up over New York City, up over the park I was thinking, with the white and red striped awning near the zoo where all the smiling nurses with babies in big fancy prams were strolling and children in little navy blazers with their school insignias on the pocket would be laughing in front of the cage where the black gorilla lounges on his elbow, with puke that smells like onions, sometimes he pukes all day and doesn't so much as even blink an eye, it just oozes out of his mouth, this thin white cream that smells like raw onions, only so strong you can't see straight for a minute when you get a whiff.

While I was lying there I was thinking how hot the room was

getting which was when the urge to talk came over me so bad, I remember I asked one of the smiling nurses how the baby was doing but no one answered.

"My baby!" I yelled.

But they still didn't say a word. They just smiled, so of course I smiled back while I was trying to figure how I could get off the litter and get over to the pay phone on the wall so I could make a crank call because at that moment I needed to make one just in order to stay alive. It was urgent to find out from whomever answered the phone how many pairs of shoes that person had. Hurry lady, I'd say if I could only get over to the pay phone on the wall—Go find out! I'll hold on, I planned to tell whomever it was—What's that? Eleven pairs you say? Not fifty? Not eighty-seven? Then I'd whisper into the receiver, Now listen carefully—you are to throw them all away right now. That's right, right this minute while I'm holding on you must go over to your closets and get rid of *every single shoe!—Do you hear?*

Who is this? Who is this calling? the lady would begin to yell.

Ah, don't worry, lady. It's okay, I'd screech as my voice would begin climbing till it became something close to platinum and glass. I love you, I'd start screaming into the telephone—I love you, lady, I'd start shrieking as the tears began.

"Two dogs ran out," I told the nurse who was holding my hand. "There was a black sports car so close on my tail I couldn't slow down or do anything but hang onto the steering wheel for my own stinking life while I left my baby standing there to die," I told her as the hospital room door opened and the head of a man popped in to ask if I wanted a priest for the baby and that's when a certain kind of hatred filled up my soul when I looked at his face, a pure, raw feeling of so much hate that must have come from utter defenselessness, I'm thinking, as I take a sip of water.

Next a policeman wearing black leather boots, a black leather jacket and a gun in a black leather case came in. "Terrible accident," I said. "Yes," he said, "a terrible accident," but I knew the word *accident* was a word we were using like a kind of life raft. What did it mean? I still wonder to this day. The word was a thin veneer, hardly even a layer at all to cover a whole universe of things that allowed me to walk away from the scene of the crime scot-free. That's what I was thinking, like I was thinking how odd it was that that policeman of all the people in the world was the person to whom I had to be accountable. Not to God or to myself or even to the baby but to a policeman whom I had never laid eyes on before in my entire life.

"Your name," he asked as he began writing in his metal-covered pad.

"Patricia Constance Marvel," I answered.

"Your age," he asked.

"Twenty-seven," I said.

"Cause of accident," he asked.

"Two big white poodles ran out from the side of the road while I was being tailgated by a little black Triumph who was so close on my back I couldn't even see his headlights. So tell me officer," I said calmly, "would you say it's murder or would you say it's involuntary manslaughter."

And that's when Alfred walked in,

"Is she dead?" I asked him but I didn't need to ask him anything. One look at his face told me, like I didn't know it anyhow. Of course I knew, I knew it all along.

I knew it in the car on the way to the hospital while I was trying to seal her neck back together with my fingers.

I knew it when I handed her with her big brown eyes wide open over to the nurse. While they were scrubbing off the blood from my legs and feet and smiling at me I knew and they knew and no one said a word. It was the secret we all shared in that hot room with the sweet smell of blood that kept us all silent and smiling at each other with Time strangely deflected, like light shooting off a mirror in the sun.

Alfred kissed my hand as he kept saying, "Thank God it wasn't you. Thank God," he kept whispering into my hair. But all I did was to keep repeating how I didn't want him to be there. I kept telling him that I didn't want to ever see his face again because I never wanted to see the kind of pain that was on his face as long as I lived.

I never once said one single word to any of them about my husband, what his name was or where he lived because I didn't want him to ever find out what happened to his child and yet there he was, red and terrible in his agony, his hair was awful, his face was ashen and there was a look of incomprehension in his eyes that I couldn't stand to look at.

I bound myself to him in the simple urge to just get going with life—The folly of it! The lark! I'm thinking as the tears start streaming down my face, Who knows anything at eighteen when I first began peeling his oranges and cutting his grapefruit sections so close there was never even the tiniest piece of pith near the meat. Every day I brought his breakfast up to him on a little silver tray that his mother gave us for a wedding gift with fresh flowers from the garden and the morning paper, and while he picked the raisins out of his raisin toast and smiled at me I was wondering to myself, Who is this man? Who on earth is this round red-faced smiling fellow with the orange sagebrush hair, the bright blue eyes and big pink freckled hands. Out of nowhere I brought a whole big bunch of things together and then, suddenly, it was my life.

It was an apple orchard out behind the garage where I used to sit with the baby in the morning.

It was a linen closet on the second floor with monograms on all the sheets and towels and pillowcases, and there were cut-crystal glasses and pink porcelain dishes and an herb garden and wild roses.

And then one day some hot-rod kid was tailgating me as two dogs ran out into the road and as they wheeled me through the big green double doors into surgery I heard a sound that was worse by far than even the one small cry the baby made. It was Alfred screaming so loud that I could hear it all the way down the hall when they took him into the room where the baby was.

"The truth is the only thing that helps."—*Alfred Marvel*

Chapter

10

*T*hey buried her in a little white casket next to old Leo Fish. Alfred stayed with me in the same hospital bed the night it happened while time danced by on little toe shoes as we lay there silently watching until the morning slipped in on a tiny gray slant from the top of the windowsill.

It took twenty-seven hours to give birth, the pain was like a tantrum, it was like a rage that went away and then came back again and each time it came back it came back harder and stayed longer. There were three crickets somewhere in the labor room I remember as I take a bite of my muffin and a sip of coffee, and between each bout of pain I would lie there listening to them making that little funny sound until the whole thing started up again. First the horns. Then the cymbals. Next came the trombones. Then the kettledrums joined in. Then they all started blasting and banging and blaring at once.

Help me! I screamed as I pulled up my knees, *Someone help me please!* I shrieked as I grabbed my feet, the sides of the bed, the sheets.

"Make them give me *something, Alfred, please*," I begged him, my face, white as the sheet with green sweat dripping in my hair. The pain was so monstrous that I couldn't believe it was happening to me.

"Take deep breaths," Doctor Lichterman said. "Push," he told me, "Push! Push! *Harder Peachy! Harder! Harder! Harder!*"

"Look," he said, "It's a girl, a beautiful little redheaded girl." "Look, Peachy," he said, "she's a carrot top just like her old man."

And then later in the dark when I was all alone with her I licked her little arms and then I sniffed her ears and neck and nose and cheeks and I nibbled on each little finger and every little toe and then I sucked on her little elbows and chewed on her soft red baby hair, so perfect all of it.

After she was killed for years I couldn't go down to the cellar or go through a tunnel or go into a dark movie theater before the show began because "dark" was where she was. I could never fall asleep without a lamp left burning in some corner of the room and I could never switch off the television set because I couldn't stand that sudden nothing when everything went black because that "sudden nothing" was where she was, so we'd leave the TV going night and day.

A train platform where the people were all jammed and waiting, the train comes tearing down the track, stops and then it silently glides off leaving the platform completely empty, everybody's gone—to *what! where?* And I'd begin to shake so bad that Alfred would have to grab me and hold me and sometimes he even had to shake me harder than I was shaking myself to stop me from the trembling.

Every time I heard the phone ring for a second I thought it was the baby calling to tell me she'd be home in fifteen minutes. Whenever the doorbell rang for a second I thought a neighbor found her and was bringing her back to us after some kind of confusing mix-up, nothing more, all of it a mistake, some incredible error because it was inconceivable to me that those four or five seconds out on Riders Road could sweep away— *everything!*

We watched the sun go down and roamed around the garden in a daze and then it was the next day and then it was night again and I would sit staring into space smoking cigarettes and waiting until five-o'clock birds were all out across a brand-new dawn and when they were, then I would finally be able to get into bed and go to sleep.

We didn't go to the funeral. Rabbi Massengil sat in the garden with us and talked about God in all His infinite wisdom and fate and everlasting peace and eternity—this thin, high-strung wild little man with his black curly hair and his thick horn-rimmed glasses and his long thin narrow hands that looked like European dinner forks, sitting on a bridge chair in front of the rosebush she helped me plant four days before.

We never wore the torn black silk of mourning and we never lit the candle the rabbi brought. We threw it in the trash the minute he left the house along with all the printed copies of his sermon that he left around for everyone to take, all of it almost a joke in the face of a loss that left me and Alfred with no place to hide, all our barriers were completely torn away so that for a long time afterwards we saw everything around us stripped down to what it really was as though a glaring light were somehow turned on to show only the Truth of Everything, making the Truth too big, and worse, without any of the trim that makes it bearable. Sometimes people get little flashes that don't take any effort, little connections and insights happen without having to even lift a finger or blink an eye—thought is weightless, it floats, sometimes hitting on the truth, but in the crush of so much unbelievable grief there was no way to shut it off. It just kept coming at us. We couldn't close a window shade even a tiny bit on the way things really were until it was like a strain of some beautiful possibility that had gone completely haywire. The daily newspaper was suddenly nothing but big bold print against white paper, Gossip! Evil! Vicious! Terrible Gossip, and on a big and hideous scale worldwide. Motorcycle cops flying off in their black helmets and black rubber goggles became human locusts eager and ready to devour everything in their wake as troops of people kept coming to our house and not because they cared about us but because they were scared and I was supposed to reassure them. That's what the mourning period became only we were so entirely without hope and since hope is the only reality, we couldn't teach them or reassure them or come up with any wisdom about the meaning of our tragedy because tragedy doesn't teach you anything because there's nothing to teach, it's just a thing that happens without any message except to say that it exists. I could have told them that she was cheated out of everything and that I was powerless to help her or I could have said that Rabbi Massengil made me numb and crazy by saying things like *God's infinite wisdom* because I didn't understand where there was any wisdom in my child's death.

A person is a magnificent creature that's caught disastrously between animal and saint. It dreams and invents and makes heavens and archangels and everlasting kingdoms. It creates what it calls eternity in its genius not to suffer. Out of its refusal to accept its own mortality it, unlike any other thing that breathes and dies, *Imagines* and has *Intentions* and *its Intentions are who it is.*

I *did not intend for my child to die and that's the only thing I could have ever told anyone.*

For months we roamed around the garden with our arms around each other while people kept coming, armies of them marching in with cookies and hard candy in dishes made of thick white hobnail china that came to be as much a part of death as lights on in the day and the dry air in there and the dusty sunlight that lay across the rug in the living room like it had been in the house for years, the sound of screen doors slamming, the sound of toilets flushing, the sound of footsteps on the linoleum floor in the kitchen, the muffled sound of voices, greetings, coughs. They whispered, they fluffed up pillows, they emptied ashtrays and drank coffee while we roamed around the garden in a daze with our arms around each other and then, on the last day of shiva, as I sat alone on the sofa before anyone came, a state of absolute peace unlike anything I ever felt enveloped me, which comes in tragedy when you accept life on its terms and not on yours, I'm thinking as I close my eyes and see that house again.

It was a big beat-up white stucco fortress behind the copper beech tree with cedars lining the drive in the back and drooping willows down beside the creek that always looked to me like a big, green lace buffalos.

You might say that house was a sort of nanny, I'm thinking as I see it again standing there with runs in its stockings and old run-down ratty shoes and its hair all loose and in a mess, but yet it endured all that weather and all those seasons that were so violent I'm thinking as I pour the last drop of cream into a fresh cup of coffee and begin to stir.

And in simply enduring it was the house most of all that taught me that Endurance must be *The Fundamental Principle!* Don't lose courage it kept saying. Don't become dispirited! Don't crumble and whatever you do, don't even think about turning in your chips. Not yet! it whispered to me time and time again like some wonderful mother who wouldn't let go for even a minute. But we left her anyhow, a mistake I'm thinking, but there were too many memories she began to wear like an old tattered shawl that finally covered everything else. Alienation, that's the word, we became alienated from her because of so much pain. The root of *alien* comes from the Latin word for "madness," so that alienation means "to be separated from one's own soul." Right, Alfred? I'm thinking.

"So what'll I do," I whisper, as I glance at my watch. "Shall I 'stick around' like he told me to do, have dinner and then spend the night with *Manuel Zot* or should I get out of here and go straight back to Vineland on the double? Please tell me what I should do," I whisper, "because you know better than anyone that I'm one of those people who never knows what to do about *anything!* Don't forget, this might be the last chance I'll ever get and he's not just anybody, remember that," I whisper. Plus if things should develop between us, I would definitely take him to Suzie Fish's wedding because I would love to show Hendella and *you* and Charlie and Loretta and Granny Heinfling a thing or two about who can have a glamorous celebrity if she wants one I'm thinking as I sip my coffee and glance at my watch.

You see, all by itself just being able to bring Manuel Zot to Suzie Fish's wedding is worth "sticking around" for because revenge is that little midnight supper of the soul. And please! Don't tell me that old single-standard line that "It's a man's world, Peachy." Because it's a new day, Alfred, ever since the pill and the Equal Rights Amendment and that whole woman's movement business. And furthermore, we're going to be divorced before the New Year and since all that's left between us are a few little parcels of real estate over in Columbus, I say, Why not?

Manuel Zot and I will have a quiet little dinner in some cozy little hideaway around Harvard Yard, nothing fancy. We'll drink wine and have a good conversation about what makes people tick, and then afterwards we'll probably go back to his place which means that for the first time in almost a year I'll be in bed with a man which would be good for me because after all, Alfred, after the baby was killed, let's face it, going to bed with me was the last thing on earth you really wanted to do. I could tell you only did it because you were stuck with me, right? So maybe we should both begin catching up on a little lost time. Or as you said, "We deserve to *live* a little," because, I'm sure it wasn't what you'd call *living*, was it, to have lost our child.

No, I guess that was something else I'm thinking as I sip my coffee and glance at my watch, like it wasn't "*living*" to have raised a child like Ruthie who was a star from the first day of her life or to have had a home to come back to every night that was orderly and clean with dinner at seven on the dot and candles always flickering on the table and our best sterling silver and a lace tablecloth every single night of the week. But I have a feeling that wasn't what you called "*living*" either. That was something else that didn't count, like it didn't count that your shirts were delivered up to your bed fresh and gleaming every Thursday afternoon as bright and as starched and as perfect as any jewel in your mother's safe-deposit box, or that every time you walked in the house the smell of what you loved to eat was always mingling with the fresh-cut flowers from our garden and the spotlessness of the floors and windowsills that were so dazzlingly clean you could have eaten off them as the days and months and years rolled along smoothly and softly with no rough edges anywhere, plus a fabulous wine cellar in the base-ment, plus only the finest stereo equipment that money could buy with nothing but Mozart going all the time, but I have a feeling that according to you that also wasn't what you called "*living*."

Every night we made it through to the following morning

with our demons under *control!* We got across Landis Avenue every time we crossed it without ever getting hit. We got through our root canal therapy in one piece, Alfred, and we made it home sick as dogs from too many tacos but we always made it home. And Alfred, when Uncle Monroe was so bad toward the end and Aunt Martha was so brave in that awful-smelling hospital room when we sat there watching the whole generation that preceded us withering as if it were autumn in the family arbor, first Aunt Lillian, then Uncle Marvel and then three months later Uncle Monroe, and you said, "Even if your mother's a total crackpot," which you were sure she was, "be kind to her," you said, "give her a break," you said, "because she did the best she could." Do you remember Aunt Martha after Uncle Monroe died, how her skin got all gray and crape-like and how big bags developed under her eyes and she got all withered and stooped like she turned ancient in less than twenty-four hours and when you looked at her you said, "So this is what love does to you. Wow!" you said, and then after you came back to the house with your dungarees sopping wet and your reindeer sweater drenched to the bone and your tan suede desert boots soaked through from the rain out at the cemetery where you went with her to select the plot, you began to cry. But, oh no, Alfred, that isn't living either, is it Alfred?

Well, I'm thinking as the tears begin to boil up in my eyes, until the day the baby was killed I did the best I could. That's right! I did the very best I could even if you didn't consider it "*living!*" And now, whatever it is you do call *living,* maybe I deserve a shot at it myself. So guess what? I think I'll "stick around"!

Forget it, Peachy, that's what you'd tell me, I'm thinking as I take a sip of coffee and glance at my watch again, in fact, you'd tell me I'm not to dare to even look at Manuel Zot. Is that clear, you'd say. And it's not so much that I even still belong to you, it's just that I *may not—period—end of report!* And then you'd turn bright red around the ears and your chin would start jerking overtime. Because of course I was a virgin when I married you, because *God forbid,* if you weren't a virgin in those days you were what Hendella called "used goods" and no man wanted that.

She really did a number on me, Alfred. African mothers do it with a knife but not Hendella, she didn't need a knife, she had her mouth that was worse than any knife because that way, efficiently, she did it to the whole person, not just to part of her I'm thinking, as I glance at my watch again.

So by the time I got married I was so afraid of everything including simply getting undressed in front of my own husband that I almost died because I never had that kind of courage in my life. In fact I had to have all the lights completely out before I even took my bathrobe off, but let's face it, when a woman stands naked in front of even her own husband, even if they've been married for thirty years, she's still taking a terrific chance.

So how in the world could I get undressed in front of *the* Manuel Zot. Not with these big boobs. And what about my appendix scar I got when I was twenty-five that goes clear across my whole abdomen with that hideous bulge at the end of it that looks like an eyelid. Oh sure, I'd really *love* Manuel Zot to have a look at that, examine it, question me about it and then start taking notes. Or how about the cellulite at the top of my thighs or my hips with their fat pads of just plain flab, and even if we got past all of that, don't forget that men want you to fiddle around with their thing or worse he might expect me to even give him a little blow job and that would really make my stomach turn because let's face it, to me a blow job is like having someone blow his nose in your mouth. So no thanks I'm thinking, *Yuk!*

And even if he didn't want me to do something like that, there's still my stomach to think about which has gotten so much wobblier than it was even five years ago. When I was only five years younger I was still what he might call passable, not a knockout, granted, but I could still make heads turn when I walked into any room at the club or when I moseyed down any street in Vineland because even as recently as five years ago I hadn't become invisible I'm thinking as tears boil up in my eyes.

Everything and I mean *everything* we cherish we lose. Women are this link between man and nature and like the seasons, everything we prize and cling to with all our strength and I mean *everything* is ripped away from us starting with our looks. Manuel Zot can have any gorgeous little creature he wants on the face of this earth, so why he wants a hag like me is the mystery of the century.

I'm an old *bag!* But that's the way it goes. That's life so face it kid I'm thinking. Even my behind which used to be okay is *finished.* Feel it, it's gotten like mush and as far as my legs are concerned, okay, so my legs are still okay because legs never change, not even when you're in your nineties, but they could stand a shave and did you bring your razor up to Cambridge—*no!* Of course you didn't, which means that in order to go to bed with Manuel Zot, author of *Robot Victory,* you'll be competing with young perfect bodies of exquisite youth and it means you'd have to get into bed in the total dark completely dressed.

And just say you were even crazy enough to take that kind of risk with your pride and with your dignity. *For what! Why, Peachy?* You mean less to Manuel Zot than this tiny muffin crumb. Famous writer or not a famous writer, celebrity, genius *and Harvard professor* all rolled into one, if it's a little bit of *kindness* you're after maybe you shouldn't turn to Manuel Zot for that because maybe Manuel Zot is just another swifty like your cousin Felix Garlich from South Orange. Anything he could get for nothing, right! as long as it was free and he could get his hands on it and it wasn't going to cost him one red cent then it was fine—great—let's go! Because after all, I'm thinking, why was Manuel Zot glaring at me like that from behind those books—why? Because he thought I was some kind of nut and nuts are always free because nuts don't have enough self-confidence to ask for anything. They're *grateful* Peachy, for even the smallest bit of attention and in fact a real nut would consider it an *honor* to be chewed up and then spit out by *the* Manuel Zot and that's why all the Manuel Zots of the world are on the lookout for just those kind of dingbats because *anything for nothing is their motto,* right? them, with their elongated thin dark slanty eyes and their loose running smiles like dripping paint that show all their pointy teeth so that they look like coyotes or maybe like a hungry wolf.

But he *is* a famous celebrity I'm thinking as I take a sip of my coffee.

But *so what,* I despise celebrities, because who the hell do they think they *are!* They're rich, selfish, spoiled and so unbelievably lucky it could make your head spin right off your neck and with all that phenomenal good fortune, instead of gratitude and enormous humility, they look down their noses at all the little people of the world who have to struggle from morning till night with all the real concerns of simply staying alive.

And what's *more,* being a celebrity is a *hoax.* Oh what poor little pathetic souls we human creatures are. We're always toting around the muffled pangs of something we lost long ago that we're always searching for from deep inside our own ancient histories that had a more than human meaning to us then when everybody was a god or a goddess and every place was our own personal Mount Olympus. All those kings and queens we have buried at the very bottom of our souls and then, one day, *bango!* we bump into a Manuel Zot and all our cooped up ancient history gods and goddesses and kings and phantoms all fly out from where we stifled them with a sob or a sigh, and immediately they latch themselves onto this Manuel Zot or to any other celebrity we see in a restaurant or on the street but they're *our* feelings, we made them, they belong to *us. It's not Manuel Zot.* It's *me,* Patricia Fish Marvel, who has imagined

Manuel Zot into the reincarnation of some long-gone love, like a certain piece of music can bring back a whole summer from long ago complete with every feeling exactly like it was, or how a whiff of perfume on a crowded elevator brings back all the agonizing love I once carried around with me for my mother, but it's *me,* my love, my tears, my needs trying to break through for just that moment's worth of sweetness down beside the little silver pond again where I sat with Leo Fish and watched the robins.

Once Alfred told me that if I squint I'd be able to see a person for what he really is. He told me squinting is a common phenomenological tool that executives use all the time before they hire someone because when you squint, he said, the truth of a person's character immediately rises to the surface. So first I have to place Manuel Zot's face firmly in my mind and then I have to squint as I'm conjuring him up signing my book in the back of WordsWorth discount bookstore.

Yes, I'm thinking and as I close my eyes I see him in my mind perfectly, and yes indeed the truth is rising to the surface—and *fast!* His face is a cold hard knot with tight lips and narrowed eyes that have icy contempt around them which gives them a measured steady glare, contempt fills in the gorges that go from his nostrils down to the corners of his lips, his upper lip is tucked around his teeth in a vicious little curl with his nostrils flaring out in loathing for anyone who wants his autograph.

Oh *my God,* I'm thinking with my eyes still shut as I'm squinting at his image in my head, art must come directly out of *rage.* In fact, the whole creative process must be propelled by nothing but pure rage *and hatred*. And what's more, he stiffed me for the check.

So answer this question, Peachy, Is this the kind of person who deserves the courage it would take to stand in front of him stark naked?

Absolutely not! Better to gather up all my belongings I tell myself, go back to the hotel, call Ruthie to make absolutely sure that everything's okay, and then leave for Vineland as fast as possible.

But wait a minute, I think, as a little wave of abject disappointment washes over me. The other side of the coin is that maybe I ought to "stick around" and say goodbye to him in a reasonable, adult and honorable way.

But *why?* I'm thinking. He already pumped me for everything I know, hit me up for the check and the next thing I know he's going to suck my blood and then take off and I'll never hear from him again for as long as I'm alive because it's all a *lie!* The whole thing, lies, lies and more *lies* and all the fakes who kill themselves trying to live them.

Get out of here, and I mean *fast!* Go home, Peachy, to where there's peace because *peace is what freedom is* I'm thinking as I quaff the last dregs in my mug, grab my bag and coat, scramble out of the booth, pay the check and run out of there.

"If you let them do it to you, you deserve it."
—*Granny Heinfling*

Chapter

11

Y*is gad-dal v'yis kad-dash sh'meh* rab-*bo,* the tinny man in an undershirt is hawking through his gigantic silver megaphone. Either he's a weight guesser or else he's an age guesser, I'm thinking as I walk as fast as I can back toward the parking lot. With each step I'm on the lookout for a place I can jump into and hide in case I run into Manuel Zot because I can't stand confrontation. My veto is not my strongest possession. Maybe one day Ruthie should give me a few little pointers on how to stand in front of someone, look him dead in the eye and then speak the truth, because I never had that kind of courage I'm thinking as an attractive man in a dark three-piece suit passes without lifting his eyes to look at me for even a fraction of a second.

So what! Big deal! I snap as the tinny man in the undershirt starts hawking through his enormous silver megaphone *Yis-bo-rach V'yish-tab-bach, V'is-po-ar, V'yis ro*-man again like kaddish is being blasted out of everywhere.

So Alfred, I'm thinking, as I stop for the light, I have to hand it to you on a couple of items. First of all you would have never stuck anyone for a check in your entire life and certainly never a woman and never for a couple of cups of coffee and a couple of blueberry muffins and some toast and juice because you were always the biggest sport and that was a very nice quality to have, and what's more, price was never an object with you either. You would have never held back because a veal chop might have cost twelve dollars, and you always ordered garlic bread which was extra, and you could always keep your mouth shut, too. Never would you have betrayed someone's confidence for any reason under the sun and certainly never under the guise of being a "writer first and a human being second." What kind of joke is that? It's backwards thinking like a completely upside-down morality.

If you had been with me today, and if you had met Manuel Zot, the two of you would have never clicked, I'm thinking as I'm walking. But it's still too bad you didn't meet him, like it's too bad you didn't get a look at Harvard Yard and at the trees with all the falling leaves on the grass and the tired lawns all around Ruthie's room in Stoughton Hall with its old oak floors and beautiful casement windows and just beyond, the Charles River with all the little sailboats, and my eyes well up as I stop for another light.

But then it's too bad about a lot of things, like about the fact that old Leo Fish never lived to see his son Charlie become chief of endocrinology at South East Regional Hospital or that our baby missed her whole life—Everything!—including going away to college with a suitcase full of beautiful dresses and high-heel shoes, and *love,* which is maybe the saddest part of all.

They always say that a mother's love is supposed to automatically sacrifice everything under the sun including herself for her child without a second thought. But I'll tell you a little secret, Alfred, the drive to stay alive is so strong that it becomes almost a reflex, like breathing or like blinking your eye when someone brings his finger toward it. If there had only been time to make a choice I know I would have made it in favor of her.

I know that's true I'm thinking as I'm walking, but in those two or three seconds which was all the time there was, an eerie calm and then some enormous impulse to hang on to the steering wheel took over everything. But it wasn't *me,* Alfred, you have to believe that. It was the *impulse!* It was the *reflex!* That's what was hanging on to that steering wheel. Because Alfred, if God had come down and if She had asked me at that moment to make a conscious *choice* I would have said for Nancy to live and for me to die. I swear, if I had only been given the choice, but, Alfred, there was no choice. And for that I have such terrible unending *shame because,* Alfred, *I wanted to live! I wanted to stay alive, Alfred! I didn't want to die! that's all, I just didn't want to die!* And for that I hate myself. So how can a marriage go on like that because it's guilt that ruins marriages, not running around or beatings or all the insults under the sun put together.

And even if you did cheat on me, even that's okay because who was I to point a finger if you found a little happiness. Who could blame you because the rules were all declared null and void out on Riders Road that day.

Oh, sure, at first I could maybe pretend to myself that nothing was going on—as I'm digging around in my pocketbook for the ticket for the car—but I had my suspicions because of that little irritation you had right under the rim of your business that never went away and what's more I caught you trying to sneak some cream on it when you thought I wasn't looking, and although I never said anything and as terrible as it made me feel at the same time—I'm thinking as I get into the car—some part of me was also relieved to know that you were finding some kind of happiness somewhere instead of all the awful pain that I had caused. So good for him, I thought, don't say a word, just let it go, I'm remembering as I back the green Cutlass station wagon out of its space.

And then, finally, one day when all the chips were stacked just right and everything was exactly in place the way it had to be, we had a good long cry together and then I said, "Okay, go. Good-bye Alfred Marvel."

And then, after you were gone, I had to pay all my own bills and I had to take care of the insurance policy and I had to understand the fuse box and know about the circuit breakers but all of that was easy beans compared to me seeing your face with that expression from the day the baby was killed and knowing for all those years that you were secretly blaming me until finally I hated to have to look at you because your eyes finally became both the judge and the jury that told me every time I looked at them that I had killed our child.

But come on, Peachy, I'm thinking, you have to forget what's unbearable. Don't hang onto it, okay. What you have to do is what Rabbi Massengil always says, "Cling only to the peace and to the fulfillment of the moment." It's all *attitude*, Peachy. Everything! And *attitude* depends entirely on what you make up your mind to *forget!* That's right, *forget!* Because in life people make the choice to either be happy or not to be happy, it's that simple. And the way they do it is based on what they decide to *forget about* because if you don't let go of certain things then you get off the track and once you're off the track then life is hell, I'm thinking as I picture Alfred's thick red bushy eyebrows and his pink neck and flaming ears and his immense skinniness and his height and how he's always been a little bit hunched over so that his head comes forward out of his shoulders like an egret or maybe like something in the stork family, and that car of his the first time I met him, the one he had in the old days that had the softest, grayest leather I ever felt, it was like butter, with the wooden dashboard and the pull-out bar, it was the most luxurious thing I had ever laid eyes on in my life.

Well, Alfred, I'm thinking as I'm cruising down Massachusetts Avenue heading in the direction of the Sheraton Commander, I spared you certain things, like I never told you about that little sound she made like the gulls when we crashed I tell his big bloated spirit that's everywhere.

To this day, that sound comes out of our refrigerator-freezer combination every time I open it. I hear it every time I use the toaster. It comes out of the fountain in the back of the house and out of the linen closet's door and out of the coffeepot. To tell you the truth I still hear that sound coming out of almost everything which was why I could never go down to the shore with you anymore. There were all those gulls down there and how was I supposed to bear it, tell me that, I'm thinking, as the two big white standard poodles and the little black sports car that was so close on my tail that I couldn't even see his front lights out of my rearview mirror, and the sun that day and the birds and the squirrels that are everywhere like they were that day when Nancy and I got into the car and even though it happened long ago it still feels like it was only yesterday.

Alfred, I'm whispering as I'm cruising down Massachusetts Avenue, I have to confess to you that I begrudge every two-and-a-half-year-old child who lives and breathes and plays down by the water's edge all her sunshine and seasons and all her tomorrows that will go on and on and on. I hate those children, like I hate every dog and bird and cat and bug that crawls the earth because they have life and my child doesn't.

As for myself, I'm still so ashamed because I wanted to live so if you still have any doubts about the woman you are lucky enough to be unloading just ask these hands that clutched a steering wheel leaving your baby completely on her own to take her chances I'm thinking as I pull into the parking lot of the Sheraton Commander where I have to pack up my things and get going as the tinny man in the sleeveless undershirt picks up his enormous silver megaphone and begins hawking *v'yis-nas-seh, v'yis-had-dor, v'yis-al-leh, v'yis-hal-lol* which I'm just beginning to realize is the little song that goes on and on and on and on forever and ever and ever and ever and ever.

"Love means sacrifice."—*Rabbi Julian Massengil*

Chapter

12

As I grab the ticket out of the automatic dispenser, slip it up behind the sun visor and then inch my way carefully onto the Massachusetts Turnpike heading south I see out of my rearview mirror great mountains of red brick buildings looming out from both sides of the highway like the wings of some gigantic bird that's flying on my tail.

America, such an incredible experiment in human dignity I'm thinking as I'm whipping along at the same clip now as all the other cars, and if this experiment doesn't work here it'll never work anywhere again on the face of this earth for all the rest of time—right, Alfred? I'm thinking as I'm flying past a white Lincoln Continental full of maybe seven Orientals.

"Land Where My Fathers Died, Land Of The Pilgrims' Pride." Yes, indeed, my fathers all died here and they were all buried here, too. All of them, old Leo Fish and his father Morris Fish and my grandfather Samuel Heinfling and his father Simon, who bought the original tract of land in Vineland, and wait a minute, Alfred, don't forget about all the Cohens on my Grandmother Heinfling's side. But still, when you get right down to it I'm thinking as I pass a black limousine, what does a Pilgrim *really* mean to me except of course Thanksgiving and all that turkey business that comes with all the trimmings and all those big family dinners we used to have at your Uncle Marvel's house, which only means being more separate than usual, so to me a Pilgrim *really* means that whole Gentile world that we could only skirt around, but never really enter because we are *Jews!* That's right! My family came from Romania, where they ate mammalgia and chopped onions and eggplants drenched in chicken fat and wore funny clothes and little woolen caps and they didn't shave and they were all dark and murky (I glance into my side-view mirror as I'm about to move out into the passing lane) and for an instant, just for that blink of an eye that's somewhere deep in the cells, the faces of hundreds of young Jewish women of Ruthie's age exactly peer out at me as they hold on to the barbed wire fence at Auschwitz and at Treblinka and at Bergen-Belsen while that same tinny man in the same white sleeveless undershirt appears in the middle of the turnpike again to start hawking through his enormous silver megaphone, *v'yis gad-dal, v'yis kad'dash,* sh'*meh ra-bo* as a new stream of tears starts streaming down my face.

Whenever we used to go to the Flyers games, right before the game began, when all the Flyers were standing solemnly in a line with their hockey sticks across their chests while we'd all be singing the National Anthem, they were right in front of me, those same faces staring at me at every marching band and parade that ever came blasting down Landis Avenue and at every Fourth of July picnic we used to have on the beach in Atlantic City when Ruthie and Suzie Fish were little or on all those summer evenings when we'd be sitting in rolling chairs on the boardwalk as the spectacle of fireworks popped and glared across the sky, those same hopeless faces hanging onto the same barbed wire fence would appear and softly whisper, *"You'll never believe what human beings can do to each other Peachy, like you'd never believe the real truth about mankind so just thank God you're in America,"* they'd whisper softly, *"just thank God every minute of your life, get down on your knees and thank Almighty God for these United States—this incredible experiment in human dignity,"* they'd whisper. I'm wiping my nose on the back of my hand as I'm flying up the exit ramp at Old Sturbridge. Ruthie Marvel's at Harvard University tonight I'm thinking, and I'm driving a green Cutlass station wagon from Massachusetts all the way down to Vineland—*imagine such a* THING! *Just I M A G I N E I T!* "Land where my fathers died, land of the Pilgrims' pride, from every mountain side, let freedom ring," I'm singing as I'm passing a Cherokee Jeep with a very old man driving two very old white-haired women.

And then my eyes fill up again. Sure, I'm thinking, for me it's a loss, and because it's sad to see Ruthie go, so sad that sometimes I can't get out of bed in the morning, each loss is like a little hole that's been cut into me and each little hole diminishes me in a way that I never really recover from but it's like what you always say, Alfred, you can't hang on to your child, *because hanging on isn't love* and, what's more, no one knows better than I that a woman feels like a failure if she lives near her mother all her life, so of course I'm telling his bloated spirit that's everywhere, I'm glad she's exactly where she is this very minute because that's life, losing *Everything* is what's called being a woman. We cook and cry and that's the way it goes. *But!* as I'm flying past the Lincoln Continental full of all the Orientals it occurs to me this brilliant hard-working beautiful young woman has earned herself permission to leave the emerald farmlands and the great Pine Barren Forest of her childhood and go *wherever* she wants to go *on the face of this earth* and become *anything she wants to become—Anything!* Because she's *free* which is something I don't know how to begin to even spell!

And for a moment, as streaks of sunlight are sparkling on the windshield of the car and the warmth of the late afternoon sun is streaming in on my face through the open window, a certain ecstatic feeling that comes with being completely alone and on one's own begins creeping up on me as tears that have to do with unbound gratitude are welling up in my eyes as I'm flying past the exit to Rockville Connecticut like the Cutlass station wagon and I are a wonderful horse and rider in some amazing race that goes on and on for hundreds of thousands of miles. And as I'm rustling around in my pocketbook for my sunglasses I'm remembering what Maxim Gorky once said, that a parent isn't successful unless her child surpasses her.

Now it's Cambridge I'm thinking and from there who knows? Maybe Paris or London or even maybe *New York City,* which in my wildest dreams I could have never dared to dream of, because from the first day of my life I knew I had to stay close to

Hendella so I could take her on all her errands or take her for her checkup like she took her mother and like my grandmother Heinfling took my great-grandmother Fanny Cohen who had the dyed red hair because that's what daughters did, those were the rules and you didn't break them like you had to be a virgin when you got married because your virginity was the most valuable thing you had and if you didn't have that then you didn't have anything or like you had to call your mother on the phone two and three times a day when you weren't carting her all over even if you had absolutely nothing to say to her but you still had to check in in the morning and check out before you went to sleep I'm thinking as I'm passing the Cherokee Jeep with the three old fogies.

Do you remember our wedding night, Alfred? How I cried and cried. For what? Why? What was I crying about? And then the next day that long two-lane highway that stretched like an endlessly boring conversation through the Pine Barrens all the way up to Lakehurst and the gloom that that highway plunged me into and how I wondered while we were driving how something as beautiful as the Pine Barrens could all of a sudden be so deadly because usually for me to be smack in the heart of nature like that would make my spirit soar because when I'm close to all that's real and therefore all that's everlasting the inner person in me usually comes alive, but not that day while we were on our way up to Lakehurst. (The white Lincoln Continental full of all the Orientals passes me.) Ah well, youth and beauty were as fleet and as ephemeral as puppyhood, nothing more, and once puppyhood is gone it's gone without a trace and then its the long hard grind of being a dog—right, Alfred?

The yen for a little something sweet, like maybe a piece of chocolate or maybe an ice cream cone begins to *tap tap tap* on all my sensibilities, that little craving for a goodie so I can stuff down everything from the pain of what I can't do a thing about anymore, to the injustice and the fury of all that's gone before, to the heartbreak over Alfred so I don't think about him or wonder where he is these days and what he's doing or who he's doing it with I'm thinking as I'm flying past the exit for Meriden Connecticut.

That lust for a sweet is like drinking blood because once you get the taste of it into your system you have to have more and more and more until you burst or fall asleep. Some kind of starvation of the spirit I guess because it doesn't have a thing to do with hunger, does it? A Sunshine vanilla creme wafer and not the thin ones either, only the thick dry ones with the thick dry icing in the middle will do, or what about something soft, ice cream and a big piece of apple pie or maybe just a plain old bag of Krispy Krinkle thick ridged potato chips. *Or,* I'm thinking, a bag of Bach's chocolate-covered peanuts that I could pick up real fast at any Bob's Big Boy (I'm flying past the white Lincoln Continental full of all the Orientals). And, if it came right down to it, I would settle in a minute for a juicy hot dog with a ton of mustard on one of those excellent hot dog rolls.

Not bad, but hold on, I'm thinking, as I'm scuffling around in my pocketbook for my box of Junior Mints. I'm going to see Alfred in less than two weeks at Suzie Fish's wedding which is a week from this coming Sunday, and since today is Thursday it means that I'm going to see Alfred in exactly ten days. And since I can't be caught looking like a big fat bloated pig, better to pass up the Big Mac and fries and instead make a mental note to call Sergio the minute I get back so I can get a haircut (the Cherokee Jeep with the three old fogies passes me). You pay most of them to humiliate you, first they wet your hair and then they comb it all the way back or else they comb it all the way forward and then to the left and then to the right till you want to die. But not Sergio.

When I was young the most popular girls were always the ones who had cropped hair and looked like boys and they were always the meanest ones too and the strongest ones I smile to myself and shake my head as I roll the window all the way down so I can see better as I move slowly out into the passing lane. Once, I bleached all the hair on my arms and legs a yellow white so I could look like all the other girls at Landis Elementary and I remember sitting on my bed and staring at all that golden fuzz on my arms and legs and for one moment in my whole life I knew what it felt like to belong. There were only a few Jews at Landis Elementary, me and Charlie and the Engleburgs, a boy in second grade named Jeffrey Farber and a dark, quiet girl whose mother hanged herself named Alice Weinrot I'm remembering as I'm approaching a long string of trucks in the far right lane. And that monster who I can still see like it was yesterday, Miss Eloise Boden, who was a fat tank in black, spinning around from the blackboard like she had eyes in the back of her head so she could catch anyone doing anything wrong, like that was the meaning of her life. To this day I can still see Alice Weinrot's face (I'm passing the first truck in the chain) the day she came into class two minutes late, *two minutes!* She tiptoed to her seat, took off her shoes, sat down very quietly so that Miss Boden wouldn't hear a thing and as she spread her dark little arms across the slant-top desk so she could put her head down for a minute and take a little rest, as if that hideous witch had some kind of device stuck in that pile of soft white hair she swung around from the blackboard *the instant* Alice Weinrot's head went down. Then she flew at Alice Weinrot and yanked her to her feet and then with her whole body weight she shoved Alice Weinrot out the classroom door and the horror on Alice Weinrot's face as she went sailing backwards with only one shoe on is something I'll never forget for as long as I live while in the back of the room Dorothy Jack was picking her nose and eating it slowly while she sat staring dumbly into space I'm remembering as I put my blinker on so I can get in to the far left lane.

Everybody hated Dorothy Jack, I'm thinking as I'm flying along now beside the first truck in the chain. They stole her pencils, they flushed her handkerchief down the toilet, they smashed the little glass weather vane her brother gave her that she kept at the bottom of her locker. And it was all because of Annie Burns and Kathleen Kuch who were maybe the meanest people that ever lived (I'm hitting seventy on the speedometer). And if you throw in Miss Eloise Boden with those secret eyes in the back of her head who was always *always!* laying in wait to catch Dorothy Jack picking her nose and then eating the boogie and the minute she did, the minute that boogie went into

Dorothy Jack's mouth and she went into her trance, *bango!* Miss Boden would spin around from the blackboard screaming *you filthy child!* and in one bound Miss Boden would grab Dorothy Jack and start shaking her and shaking her until Dorothy Jack began to rattle and her little mouse eyes fell out on the ground. Then Miss Boden made Dorothy Jack go up to the front of the class and stand up there in front of everyone and recite her prepositions. And that's when Dorothy Jack began to stutter, Dorothy Jack began to hiccup. She began making sounds like a monkey or a hippo because she was a bad stutterer and Miss Boden knew it like everybody knew it, we all knew she couldn't stand up there in front of everyone and speak even though she knew all her prepositions perfectly. But Miss Boden pushed her up there anyhow while the whole fourth grade watched, our eyes glued in a weird fascination to so much cruelty I'm remembering as I'm rustling around for a couple more Junior Mints.

Memory must begin in connection with other people; what they've done to you, what you've done with them, faces, hands.

What do people long for and what does a person mourn more than the loss of an even nightmarish childhood. We sang of Christ. We sang of the Savior. Sweet children's voices filled the music room. One and two, and one and two, Miss Stedly led the singing backward from the upright. One and two, and one and two, her fat arm with the pink gold watch on a thin black band slicing the air behind her back while we sang of the Lord. We sang of peace and of joy and of Jesus born to Mary who was chosen by God.

Dorothy Jack wasn't out at recess time. She had to stay inside and sit for that hour on the finger she used for picking her nose. For a long time after I thought about her and what I saw and what it was like to see it and then in twelfth grade an English teacher accused me of plagiarizing a story I had written for an English composition class and for me that was the beginning of the end. (I pass the Cherokee Jeep with the three old fogies). The fact was that I wrote the first draft of that story in less then twenty minutes on the back of the Number Four bus on my way home from school which I swore up and down till I was on the verge of tears. But it meant less than nothing I'm remembering as I dig out another Junior Mint—I even made the mistake of confiding to the English teacher that my closest friend had recently moved away and since then nothing had mattered at all, and that writing that story really got me going again. And, in fact, I told her I not only forgot my troubles while I was writing it but I became actually happy, and since being happy isn't ever so easy to come by it meant to me that maybe writing was something I should think about because when something makes you happy it's an indication that whatever it is is right for you because how else can you tell, I asked her, what other sign do you have about a really important thing except how happy it makes you? But as I looked at her face I could tell that what I said didn't mean a hoot. I could tell that nothing I said mattered one bit and that the truth was of so little concern to her that she couldn't care less about even listening to me. And as far as my theory about the best way to understand yourself, which is via happiness, that was also nothing as far as she was concerned— the fact was, I was baring my soul to a monkey or to a rock and what was even more sinister was that this *thing*, this less than human creature, had the power to kick me out of Vineland High School at the beginning of twelfth grade if I didn't tell her where I stole the story. That's what she was telling me as she was pushing me by the shoulder toward the principal's office where she informed me, as she was pushing me along, that my twelfth-grade advisor, the principal *and Hendella Fish* were all *waiting* for me.

As I'm digging out the last of the Junior Mints I'm remembering the fact that I never stole a thing in my entire life and that I didn't lie or cheat and that I not only loved writing that story but the idea of writing was a whole new world for me, which is what school's supposed to be all about, but it meant nothing (I pull out into the left lane in order to pass another truck). So the whole time I was in the principal's office I felt like I was going to pass out cold while the little mole of a principal who had one normal eye and one big black gray one that never moved, it just stared at you all the time like a big dead headlight, while the English teacher who looked like a pelican dressed all in blue with blue-white hair and a big blue cape over an identical matching blue wool dress and silver earrings that were so heavy they stretched the holes in her earlobes all the way down, and the twelfth-grade advisor who was a mean little weasel with thin gray lips, were all grilling me on where I got the story while my mother looked like she was going to pass out, too (I'm flying along in the far left lane in order to pass all the trucks). They were all so full of hate that they couldn't even put their fingers on what they hated anymore, just that they hated everything but

I didn't know that at the time. At the time I figured I had somehow done something terrible only I didn't know what it was that's what I was thinking as the principal finally told Hendella that of course she knew all along where I stole the story . . . *Kipling!* She smiled and as I sat there listening it all began to spin, the whole thing, them, the room, the sound of their voices, last summer, Annie Weiss and I in the high grass behind my grandfather's house, the new yellow dress my grandmother had just gotten me to wear to my cousin Naomi Cohen's wedding—around and around it all was spinning along with all the plants on the windowsills, the principal's desk and her one dead eye as I sat there shaking my head from side to side real fast to help me from passing out and that's when it dawned on me that the only possible solution to the problem was Leo Fish! *Of course,* because after all he was a big professor at the Rutgers University School of Medicine, a famous thoracic surgeon in New Jersey and, true, he went completely off his rocker if someone dared to eat butter in front of him but other than that he was famous for being very smart because he was not only Phi Beta Kappa in College but in medical school he was Alpha Omega Alpha and you couldn't do much better than that on the face of this planet. Plus my father was also a big shot in Vineland because he operated on everybody who was anybody in that whole community for over twenty years including the chief of police, the mayor, every racketeer and politician and all their relatives. Sometimes the phone rang all night; broken legs, stomach pains, puking blood. "Doctor Leo Fish, Surgeon" the brass plaque read and from the milk-brown waiting room with

all the *National Geographic* magazines and all the *New Yorkers*
in a pile and the dim little lamps with their heartbreaking little
parchment lamp shades, a door would open and you'd see the
white starched coat buttoned sharply over his paunch, the big
smiling teeth, yellow from too much coffee, the broken nose
that was finally resolved into the shape of a fat strawberry. And
all the bragging about all his wealthy patients, "Thoroughbreds"
as he called them, stunned by their bank accounts and by the
humiliating little gifts they sent him, two tickets to the circus,
two pounds of lobster meat or an electric shaver. His office was
attached to our house so I always used to see them, the rack-
eteers, the gangsters, the airline hostesses, thin scrawny
women with bleached yellow hair in big pink rollers, neat frilly
Italians, old men who looked like birds, pip-squeaks, sailors,
hot shots. Some looked like bugs, some looked like cows, some
looked like little weasels or porcupines. I hated to go in there
because they'd all glare at me and that used to scare me, and
anyhow, as far as my father was concerned, he had a temper and
he was a terrible prude. No dirty words ever, no belching, no
farts, which he called "escapes," or God help you! The man
never had an itch so I never saw him scratch around in his life
and neither could anybody else. As far as I was concerned he
was also a split personality. Outside the house, like in his office
or at a party or on the street when he'd run into people he was all
smiles and charm but once inside the house all hell broke loose
like he purposely saved up all his venom to blast on us. Our
house was much too big to air condition so in the summer it was
like a swamp in there but even if it was a hundred degrees

outside Leo Fish always wore a jacket and a vest and a tie and a white oxford button-down shirt to dinner every single night of his life. And every night all bundled up to his chin he'd sit there waiting for someone to God *forbid* eat the butter that was on our little silver butter plates. In fact you couldn't even look at the butter because butter made him crazy, so why Hendella kept putting it on the table every night was one of the great unanswered mysteries of my life. But all of that aside, I'm thinking as the white Lincoln Continental passes me, he was the only one who could get me out of the terrible thing that was happening so I had to get to him I remember thinking as I looked at my mother was who so humiliated she couldn't look me in the eyes and that's when I knew, when I looked at her listening to the three of them, that it was too late. Their minds were made up which meant that they'd never let me speak or let Hendella speak or let Leo Fish or his whole team of thoracic surgeons or even the whole medical school of Rutgers University say a word on my behalf. In fact it was all settled before Hendella and I even walked into that room that I was a dirty little stinking cheat and that was that, the ball game was over, we could stand on our heads till the cows came home because *they didn't care!*

So what should I do now, I remember I was thinking—*tell me that, so tell me what I should do! Pull out all my hair* I remember I was thinking *or maybe I should rip off all my clothes and then start shouting in some never before heard-of language or better yet maybe I should just go bang my head against the wall until I'm dead because this is the way the world is Peachy, so just get used to it—OKAY!*

And then all of a sudden it hit me like a ton of bricks that maybe all of this was happening to me as a punishment for the bad thing I had recently been doing on the bus. After I finished some of my homework, which usually didn't take very long like the story only took twenty minutes to get it all down, I'd put my books under my coat on the seat beside me so no one could sit there and as we were flying up Almond Avenue I'd close my eyes and then I'd lower my head all the way down to my knees and then I'd begin to imagine the wet sopping strands of black hair hanging in the face of my friend Annie Weiss who moved away and as I crossed my legs and then pressed down very hard on the wooden slatted seat as the bus was bumbling up Wilkens Drive, and if I squeezed my legs together very tight and then if I leaned all the way forward and if I grabbed my legs in my arms and if I held my breath as the bus flew up over Landis Avenue, electric waves that began in my vizzy would turn into waves and waves of rolling ecstacy, coming and coming over and over and over and over as we bumped and jangled and then tore up Northwest Boulevard. So as I sat there in the principal's office, staring at Hendella who I loved so much, as I looked at her hands clasped in her lap and the knot her mouth was pulled up into and her eyebrows that were crossed like two little caterpillars with two terrified eyes gazing out from under them I began swearing to God on everything that was holy that if they didn't kick me out, as God was my holy witness never again as long as I lived would I ever *ever E V E R* do that business on the bus again— *It was over!* I sat there swearing *completely and entirely over!*

From that moment on it would never ever happen again so help me God! I was vowing and swearing and promising and praying.

Hendella talked too much. That was her biggest problem (I get back into the right lane as the white Lincoln Continental full of all the Orientals passes me). If she was in a tight spot or if she was just plain nervous or if she had to go to the dentist or if she was around new people whom she wasn't completely sure about, her mouth would turn on like a spigot and there was nothing anybody could do until it ran its course. First she would start bragging about how much money and servants and cars and jewels her grandfather Simon Heinfling had "amassed" as a pioneer in the chicken industry. And then she would start dropping names, like Ty Cobb once had dinner with her father, and they were familiar with the Palestinian volleyball team who had once been houseguests in her father's home when she was growing up while her hands were rolled into two little fists in her lap and her cheeks were flushed a light crimson because she was nervous and afraid.

We were in a terrible jam, and worse, she didn't doubt for a minute that what they said about me was the God's honest truth (I'm passing the exit to Waterbury Connecticut) because my mother had a way of believing anything anybody in authority said about anything and the last person who spoke was the one she'd listen to, no questions asked. And add to that the fact that they were all Gentiles and that automatically threw her into an even worse tizzy. *What's the matter with you? This is their school,*

Peachy, I can still feel her eyes glaring at me from the other side of the principal's office.

Like *This is their world or don't you know that yet?* her eyes were scorching. *You and I and all the other dark little trolls who scurry around the edges are only renters here. We are not owners Peachy! We go to their schools because they let us! We farm their land because they let us. We go to their Acme Supermarket, fly their flag, sweep their sidewalk, pay their taxes, join their army, bribe their policemen with a little gift at Christmas and are still alive today because they, thank God, have let us live another day and still another day after that.* And this little secret unmentionable attitude of hers was stamped so deeply into every cell of Hendella's being that to my own mother even I was nothing more than some lousy little Jew who got caught stealing a story for an English composition class.

I remember like it was yesterday her finally clearing her throat and then saying, "Ladies, I do have something to tell you that's *very* important." And then she cleared her throat again and said, "With my own two eyes, these very eyes that are looking at you now, I saw Patricia write that story at our kitchen table while I was mending the ruby crystal vase that my great-grandfather Rudolph Heinfling brought back from Austria for my grandmother as an engagement present over seventy-eight years ago. I can tell you as God is my holy witness," she said, "that with my own two eyes I saw my daughter write that story from scratch. And I can tell you also, in fact I can swear to you on a stack of Bibles, that not one single word of that little story was copied from anything. In fact," she said, as she beamed a big fake smile at me as I sat there dumbfounded, "I had to tell Patricia from time to time how to spell maybe thirteen words. And I also must tell you that this child labored over that assignment all evening long. She would sit there writing and then staring into space and then she'd write some more and then she'd stare some more so that the story took hours to write and I mean *hours.*"

Then I saw them all silently moving around, I saw coats coming out and going on, and then I noticed everybody was standing up and nodding to each other but my ears were completely dead. And as the brittle little one-eyed principal held the door open for us I remember my head was throbbing like a drum and that I couldn't swallow because I was so numb and dumbfounded and under it all the whole time I had the maniacal feeling that I wanted to kill my mother.

Oh no! Not that I actually wanted her to be dead, God *knows!* (I'm passing the Cherokee Jeep with the three old fogies) but I still wanted to strangle her with my own bare hands. That's what I was thinking as she and I walked down the long wooden hall in silence and then down the long wooden stairs to the first floor and then down another long wooden hall toward the big front door. And the whole time we were silently walking my head was spinning and my mouth was like the whole Sahara Desert while I kept having a maniacal urge to choke Hendella with my own bare hands until all the lies and her tongue and her eyeballs would all fall out on the floor and then, that way, I could jump up and down on them and desecrate them exactly the way she had desecrated me.

Only, as usual, she beat me to the punch because once we were finally outside in the sunshine again and when she was absolutely sure we were completely out of anybody's earshot, with a look on her face like she was going to choke me with *her* own bare hands, she grabbed me by the shoulders and started shaking me while she yelled, "*Okay Peachy, you just better tell me where you stole that story or I'll break your neck—do you hear? Where did you get that story from?*

On the bus, the last thing I wanted to see was her face then or ever, because to me from that time on she was just like all the rest of them so I had to keep saying as I sat next to her, *Know always that you are not like those people, Peachy, and know that you must separate from people like this, mind and body, and know that even if it means you have to be alone for all the rest of time, then okay, you'll just have to be alone,* I kept repeating over and over, because it was all over for me, school, her, and little did I know at that moment, my whole future as well.

When she got off the bus to catch the Public Service for Cherry Hill to do some errands for my grandmother I didn't so much as even nod good-bye to her. I just got up without even looking in her direction, I went all the way to the back of the bus, sat down, and as I put my books and my coat on the seat beside me, without making any apologies to God for any promises broken I started thinking about how Annie Weiss and I used to watch Jeffrey Farber through a pair of her father's binoculars as he walked around his bedroom naked. And as the bus started up again I crossed my legs, bent over, grabbed them in my arms and as I lowered my head all the way down and leaned even more forward and then pressed down hard on the wooden slatted seat as the bus began to rattle up Northwest Boulevard those same ecstatic waves began coming and coming, over and over again and again and again for what seemed like minutes.

When I walked into the house I heard Hendella telling Leo Fish the whole story. The two of them were in the living room and since I didn't feel like going through it anymore I tiptoed quietly through the dark front hall toward the stairs when all of a sudden my father was charging me like a human bullet. I never said a word in my own defense because he never gave me a chance. I just stood there listening to him ranting and yelling and screaming while I was thinking that he, of all people, should not be doing a thing like this to me because he, of all people, should know *who I am*. But he was going at me like he'd lost his mind. So I just stood there staring at him while he kept yelling and then, finally, I started walking toward the stairs. Let him yell, I've had enough I was thinking as I went up to my room, slammed my door as loud as I could and then headed straight for my bathroom to have that fatal cigarette.

In those days the bathroom was the only place in the whole house where I was absolutely sure I'd find a little peace and quiet. So in I went, locked the door, opened the window all the way and before I even took out my pack of Pall Malls, which I kept hidden underneath the bathtub, I wet my washcloth, wrung it out, sprinkled Listerine antiseptic mouthwash on it and put it on the window sill. Then I sat down on the radiator in front of the open window, took out a cigarette, lit it, picked up the washcloth with the Listerine antiseptic mouthwash on it and as I sat there smoking in front of the open windows, with my left hand I started waving the wet washcloth with the Listerine antiseptic mouthwash in the air to absorb any traces of smoke and that's when I heard the first knock on my bathroom door. "Who is it?" I asked, as I doused the cigarette in the toilet, flushed it down and then stood in front of the closed toilet bowl in abject terror. Then came the second knock. "Who is it?" I asked again as I turned on the shower to get a blanket of steam going as I began waving the washcloth with the Listerine antiseptic mouthwash as fast as I could. And that's when I heard another knock and then another, so I turned off the shower, closed the windows, flushed the toilet again, shoved the pack of Pall Malls into the pocket of my gray flannel shirt, took a deep breath and opened the door.

There he was alright, his face ashen with rage as he pushed past me. He was so furious he could only sputter as he grabbed my robe off the hook behind the bathroom door and went through the pockets. Then he plowed through everything in my medicine chest, the toothpaste, the aspirin, the skin scrub, all my lipsticks, my deodorant, my face powders and rouges and all my eyeliners that were in a little plastic cup, then he looked behind the toilet. Nothing! Next he got down on all fours and looked under the sink and the bathtub. Nothing again! Then he looked in the crack between the bathtub and the wall. Still nothing! (I glance in the side-view mirror so I can pull out and pass another truck.) It was like watching someone with his shoes on fire or someone who had sizzling embers in his Jockey shorts. He was jumping and hopping all around as he was feeling the top of the wainscot with a weird look on his face. Vineland's great thoracic surgeon, *the* professor of medicine at Rutgers had gone completely crackers and why I'll never know. All I knew was that one wrong blink of my eye or one wrong twitch of my lower lip and it would be all over for me, because Leo Fish knew how to size up every situation like how my hand that was clutching the Pall Malls was wiggling slightly in my pocket, so of course he grabbed me and in one jerk my hand and the pack of cigarettes went flying out.

My father had a furiousness where it came to me. I didn't have to do anything but just be there and he'd go insane with rage. His hand came flying through the air and whammed me *Crack!* so hard across the cheek that to this day if I press it there it hurts I remember as I'm shoring myself up on the inside all over again in order to withstand the blow exactly like I did that afternoon.

Never in ten million years would Alfred ever do a thing like to Ruthie. *Never!* I'm thinking. Oh sure, he might have given her a dirty look if he had to, *maybe!* And once he pulled the phone out of the jack and shook it at her because she had been on it three hours nonstop but that was *it!* Because *who does a thing like that? Where does it come from,* I'm asking as I'm speeding along.

And what's more, he never even asked for my side of the story about what happened in school, not one word! He of all people who was supposed to stand for something I'm thinking as I'm digging around to see if I can find one last Junior Mint. He was as bad as Hendella and that little one-eyed principal and the twelfth-grade advisor and the English teacher all rolled into one because at least they didn't hit me—I glance into the side-view mirror, pull out, get into the far left lane and give it the gas.

And if that were only the end of it but it was only the beginning.

That night at dinner he bolted up from his chair in the middle of his lamb chop, turned to my mother, opened his mouth as if to say something to her only instead of saying anything, he dropped his fork so naturally as I bent down to pick it up for him I was expecting all hell to break loose all over again. Here it comes, now we get the punishment for lying at Vineland High School about cheating on my English paper, for smoking, for how I always gave him dirty looks and that I was fresh and that I didn't study as hard as I was supposed to and that I never combed my hair back neatly anymore or used the sterling silver barrettes he bought me, which I knew was the way he wanted me to wear my hair and worse, I was even threatening to cut it off which I knew he absolutely forbade, my room was a mess, I always left the lights burning all the time—didn't I know it cost a fortune to leave lights burning—what was I—dumb? But that night he didn't do anything at all. He just stood there staring at my mother with both hands clutching the top of his head. Then all of a sudden he slithered down to the floor beside his chair and as my mother and brother ran to him as he was lying there staring up at the ceiling I flew out of the dining room.

I remember running in the dark through the house, and then in my bedroom I remember crouching in the corner in the dark, and while I was listening to the sirens and watching the red flashing lights against my black bedroom wall I was praying and promising and vowing and swearing to God Almighty that if my father would be alright I would never *ever* as long as I lived do that business on the bus again. It was *over!* And this time for *good* I was pleading and begging if God would only let my father be alright. But he wasn't alright. It was a stroke.

When he came out of the hospital a dead hand hung down on his hip like an inflated rubber glove. He couldn't speak. He couldn't tie his shoelaces, button his shirt or cut his meat. In the beginning he never even came downstairs even for dinner and for over a year he never put his foot out the door. My job was to give him his shot of insulin first thing in the morning before I went to school as he sat in his three-way leather chair with the smell in that room of diabetes, Wildroot Creme Oil greased into his hair, newspapers all over the floor from the night before and his feet.

It was a rotting sweet fruity smell that never went away no matter how long we aired out the room or vacuumed in there or wiped down all the woodwork with Mister Clean. The smell stayed until it became a part of our lives like the dark must become part of a coal miner's vision or the way the deafening sound of machinery must somehow attach itself to a factory worker forever. When he went over to the dresser to scribble down some instructions for me he would walk like there was an invisible person lifting his right leg up and then setting it down for him again. His right eye drooped and his mouth on the right side dribbled spit and most of the time he didn't even know it (I'm passing the white Lincoln Continental full of all the Orientals). For his dead arm Doctor Sasson gave him a rubber ball to squeeze five times a day but other than that all we could do was try not to aggravate him because even the slightest thing like me whistling in the bathroom, could send his blood pressure soaring. And even though Dr. Sasson said there was one chance in ten that maybe he could get back some of his faculties—maybe!—chances were even greater that one of these days he'd have another stroke because his blood pressure would shoot sky high over almost anything making his blood pressure like a time bomb ticking in his head and to make matters even worse, his bedroom stank to high heaven because he wouldn't take even half as much insulin as Dr. Sasson said he needed. And why? Because Leo Fish *was the DOCTOR wasn't he and he knew everything* didn't he? And no one argued with him anymore, we wouldn't dare.

I'm so *sorry,* Daddy I'm sobbing as I'm wiping my nose on the back of my hand as I'm remembering the flowers that kept coming after it happened until the house started looking like a funeral parlor. Everybody in all of New Jersey must have sent flowers to old Leo Fish until we didn't know where to put them anymore. And the presents. And the food. His patients made cakes for him and cookies and pies. Someone sent him a jigsaw puzzle of New York Harbor I'm remembering like it was yesterday (the Cherokee Jeep with the old man driving the two old ladies goes flying past me) someone sent him a pair of yellow drip-dry shortie pajamas, someone sent him a navy blue snap-on bow tie with big white polka dots. But all his presents stayed in their boxes on the card table in front of the big bay window in his bedroom with their little notes tucked neatly in the tissue paper.

He wasn't interested (the white Lincoln Continental full of all the Orientals passes me) like he wasn't interested in the little rubber ball he was supposed to squeeze for at least a half an hour twice a day. But no, he was the doctor, so of course he did it when he felt like which meant that sometimes a whole week would go by without him even looking at the little rubber ball, or else he'd go at squeezing it like he was in training for the Goodwill Games and that was always a disaster (I pass the Cherokee Jeep with all the old fogies) because the fingers on his right hand didn't move at all. His right hand was like a dead crab that was attached to the end of his arm so that every time he'd try to pick up the ball and couldn't, he'd get so furious that with his left hand he'd grab the teapot on the card table and heave it against the wall or else with his left arm he'd sweep the card table clean sending all the presents with all their little notes flying. Or else, when he was really bad, he'd grab his dead arm with his left hand like it was a piece of driftwood and then he'd start banging it and banging it over and over and over again against the card table until Hendella would go flying in there like the house was on fire and she'd start shrieking and screaming at him. That's how she handled him, no sympathy I'm thinking as the tears are streaming down my face. She'd let him have it so bad sometimes my hair stood up I'm remembering as

I'm passing the white Lincoln Continental with all the Orientals. And then came the shoe brace and that was the last straw for old Leo Fish. It was a big ugly contraption that opened down the front with two big metal supports on each side, and there were leather straps with buckles and thick soft padding with a high leather shoe attached by a thick metal bar under the sole, and after that thing went on his leg there was no more rage, no more frustration, no more fits, no more anything. He just sat there staring blankly into space locked forever into his hideous shoe contraption. From then on, whenever I went in there either to close a window or to bring him in his breakfast or to give him his shot of insulin before I went to school in the morning, he would simply turn his head away so as not to have to look at me. We were finished—kaput!

After the shoe contraption nothing between us existed, not even an angry look. It was all over between me and the big dark man who used to take me with him everywhere he went like we were the Golddust twins.

When I was little he bought me all my clothes and took me to Woolworth's five-and-dime every Saturday for all my jewelry. It was our ritual after he finished washing the car. Then on Sunday, first he'd take me out to breakfast and then over to visit my Grandfather Fish who lived in Rosenhayn and my father and I would sit on bridge chairs in a big gloomy room where there were maybe thirty bridge chairs all lined up like in a movie theater in front of a small-screen television set and no one uttered a single word, not one sound came out of any of us until Leo Fish and I got up to leave and that's when my Grandfather

Fish slowly got up, too, took a huge wad of cash out of his trouser pants pocket, peeled off a few bills, crumpled them into a ball, pressed the ball silently into my hand and then squeezed my fingers so tight around the bills it hurt as he nodded to me as if to say hello—fine—yes—come again—okay—good-bye all rolled into one. He was a bootlegger although everyone in the family said he was in the coat front business and after my grandmother died he developed affiliations with the racetrack in Atlantic City where he got involved with betting. He lived on vanilla milk shakes, Hellmann's mayonnaise on white bread and birthday cake which gave him the secret obscene strength of a gorilla and more than anything on the face of this earth I despised kissing him (the white Lincoln Continental full of all the Orientals goes flying past me) because he gave fat, soft, warm wet kisses right on the lips that used to make my stomach turn. He was big with white hair on his head and it grew out from the tops of his shoulders like a cactus plant and it hung down under his armpits like Spanish moss and it was on the tops of all his fingers and in his ears and it shot out of his nose.

Morris Fish, I'm thinking, in his white cotton elastic waistband trousers with his white short-sleeved sport shirt and his white suede loafers with no socks and his high gloss fingernails. He used to call me "daughter" because he wasn't sure if I was Peachy or if I was Uncle Willie's daughter Rita, wonder where he is these days, in Heaven or is he a goat in the Andes now, or is he just plain dead and buried in Har Nebro Memorial Park along with his son old Leo Fish, and his son Willie, and his son Barney, and his son Packey, who saved my life when I was little with a blood transfusion that they took directly out of his arm and put directly into mine. Sometimes I think I see all of them at the Shop Rite over in Newfield along with Grandfather Heinfling and my cousin Robbie Garlick from South Orange who got run over when he was seven years old, all those old familiar faces that one day just plain vanished off the face of the earth forever, maybe they're all a school of salmon now, or a parliament of owls I'm thinking as I roll the window up because it's getting a little nippy.

On our way to visit Morris Fish, my father would always pull my nose and honk the horn of his big black Oldsmobile at exactly the same moment, or else he'd pull my ear and whistle at exactly the same instant which used to make me laugh so hard I couldn't see straight and besides all the fun we used to have there were all those hoodlums I used to love who used to hang around in front of my grandfather's house like Anatole Steinbrink who had some kind of rare blood disorder, so before we went up to sit silently in that gloomy dark front room, my father would press down on all of Anatole's fingernails, then he'd look up Anatole's nose with his flashlight, then he'd stand behind Anatole and go all the way down both sides of Anatole's neck with his fingers as he'd stare at the sky, then he'd slap Anatole Steinbrink on the back to indicate that everything was fine, and with that Anatole Steinbrink would walk me up and down the sidewalk on the tops of his shoes while my father began peeling off bills to a dapper little midget they called "The Greek" who drove around in a long blue Cadillac that was always parked in front of my grandfather's house.

There was "Fat Tubby," who hippelled around out there like the mayor of the group, this giant monster, who must have weighed four hundred pounds, would grin while he picked his teeth with the torn off corner of a hundred-dollar bill. And "Eight Cents" Goldberg and "Little Georgie Scooter" and "Yonk," who posted bail, and "Jake the Fake" Rabinowitz, who tap-danced around on the sidewalk while he snapped his fingers and smacked his hands together real fast to make a funny little clacking sound while "Approximately" Metzman would sidle up to my father like an eel, grin and then slip out a hand to shake like his hand was a secret weapon. "How many points today, huh Doc?" he'd whisper. And my father in his brown Borsalino hat cocked sidewise on his enormous head, his brown hand-stitched vicuña coat from Jacob Reed's in Philadelphia and his beautiful brown Italian leather gloves would point to the little midget to indicate that "business" was already taken care of. (I pass the Cherokee Jeep.) We always used to go to the movies on school nights, just the two of us. He was the one who'd always take me on the shooty shoots at the fair they had every year at the school for feeble-minded girls I'm smiling as I'm flying past the white Lincoln Continental full of all the Orientals. Our rickety little car would go slowly, slowly, up, up, up the big green paper Alps, higher and higher and higher. "Hold on, Peachy" he'd shout, "hold on," he'd yell, "hold on," he'd scream as we suddenly came ripping, tearing down the other side shrieking and laughing.

But somewhere along the way I must have done something terrible only I don't know what it was or even when it happened.

People need reasons I'm thinking, and undoubtedly they exist, but I was never smart enough to figure out what I did. All I know is that one day he started complaining to Hendella that I had runs in my stockings or that my slip was showing and this made him crazy. Or else he complained that I shot him dirty looks and snapped at him and he even told Annie Weiss that I wouldn't kiss him anymore or give him a little hug or sit on his lap like I used to do. And on top of that he always barged into my bedroom without knocking and then he'd just stand there with a dumb, stunned, goofy look on his face which scared the day-lights out of me so I'd start screaming for my mother who'd take me aside and whisper that he was a very sick man, didn't I know he had very high blood pressure with diabetes thrown in plus he had a bad bursitis in his right shoulder that gave him terrible pain. And then she'd stare at me without blinking, which meant that I could help out a little, not hinder, by just being a little bit more affectionate to him because he was complaining lately to her that I had turned into a pickle who was giving him the cold shoulder all the time but *oh no!* Hendella would glare at me, instead of my helping out by being sweet I left lights on *all day long* and in a house the size of ours it cost a fortune plus I was never off the phone for a minute, I ate butter in front of him which I knew he hated, but did that stop me? *No!* And why did I insist on cracking my chewing gum when I knew it drove him crazy and with his high blood pressure which of course I knew he had, cracking gum was like pointing a loaded gun directly at his brain, but even that would be alright she said if I would only kiss him once in a while and from time to time give him a little hug, what was the big deal? or go out to the movies with him like I used to do. And it wouldn't kill me either to sit on his lap from time to time for old time's sake like maybe twice a month and even if I had to fake it, she said, then I should fake it, because after all it was only being "nice," she said.

But after the shoe contraption I'm thinking as I pass the Cherokee Jeep, I didn't so much as exist to my father anymore. When I went in there in the afternoon when I came in from school there were no runs in my stockings, my slip wasn't showing and I never pulled a face on him again in my entire life. The first minute I was in his room I'd kiss him on the forehead and put my arm around his shoulder and then I'd kiss him on the forehead again as I breathed through my mouth because he stank to high heaven of warm Liederkrantz so bad it made my stomach turn. But never mind all that I'm thinking as the white Lincoln Continental full of all the Orientals passes me, I did it anyhow. He'd be sitting in his three-way leather chair in his navy blue silk bathrobe with a yellow ascot around his neck and the shoe contraption on his right leg while his left leg was so white and hairless in a brown leather bedroom slipper that it looked like it belonged to someone else, but the instant he laid eyes on me, before I was even completely in the room, he'd turn his head away. He'd be sitting with Doctor Sasson who came every day to pay a visit, his dead arm would be stretched out on the card table between them like a display of what happens to a person who has a child like me and not a word—not a nod— *nothing! Not even a glance.*

Talk to me! Say something! Anything! Daddy! P L E A S E!! But no! Not a sound came out of him and there was no expression on his face, because I wasn't there as far as my father was concerned. I didn't exist anymore.

When I gave him his shot of insulin in the mornings he'd stare blankly at the television set, his eyes not even blinking and when I said good-bye I was going to school he wouldn't turn to look at me except once in a while I'm remembering as my eyes fill up. Sometimes out of a clear blue sky, he'd bolt out of his three-way leather chair and with that quick bird look on his face he'd start tapping his breastbone as he tried to pronounce his name which was to let me know in case I should ever forget that once Doctor Leo Fish could do the rumba, the samba and the mambo, walk six miles every day, read French almost as well as he could read English and use the long pincer fingers of his dead right hand so fast and so delicately that everyone in the State of New Jersey said that he was maybe the best thoracic surgeon in the world.

Coming home from school I'd see him sitting on a beach chair in front of Lacey's Delicatessen which was on the busiest corner in Vineland, a corner that for some reason attracted every character in all of South Jersey, and even though Lacey's carried a full line of groceries and truly wonderful produce as well as having a decent enough deli, it was a clip joint because the pears and the apples were exactly double the price they would be anywhere else and not only that I'm remembering as the truck behind me starts flashing his lights so he can pass, in the back was a shelf of exotic items like pickled watermelon rind and jars of kumquats and imported Greek olives in little fancy bottles that looked like they were real blown glass, but the prices of those items were so astronomical that nobody ever bought them and even after years of being on that shelf Mr. Lacey never reduced the price. And besides all that, I'm thinking as I get back into the far right lane so the truck can go, the smoked fish except for the Nova sometimes tasted a little like camphor, some of the kaiser rolls were like rocks so you had to feel around, the cold cuts very often were slick when you got them home, the price of their imported Swiss cheese was hilarious, the noise in there was horrible, the place stank of pickles and onions so bad you couldn't breathe, all the waitresses were crabs and Mr. Lacey was a wizened old lunatic who mumbled curses as he swept the pavement all around where my father had his beach chair. The only good thing about that place I'm thinking as I'm flying along again were all the characters, drug dealers and addicts, deadbeats, hoodlums, bookmakers, numbers writers and always a bunch of bohemians from the poetry center in Elmer complete with their black eye makeup and their black clothes and black stockings and black hats and black shoes like they were all in mourning for something they couldn't exactly put their finger on.

And on that sidewalk in front of Lacey's big glass door, in a yellow and green and white striped plastic beach chair with a Yellow Pages phone book under the leg with the shoe contraption, his dead arm resting in his lap like a sleeping pet, a black beret at a jaunty angle to the side of his enormous head and an ascot tucked into the neck of his pink oxford shirt like the men on the covers of fashion magazines, was my father. As I'd come around the corner I'd say hello to him but he'd never nod to me because as far as Leo Fish was concerned I didn't exist. So finally I figured, okay, you win. If that's the way you want it, the best thing I can do is take the hint. After all, I was thinking, since I was the one who got him into this, since I was responsible for what had happened to him even though Hendella and Doctor Sasson swore up and down that it was strictly a medical disaster because he had extremely high blood pressure all his life, but since I knew the truth no matter what they said, and since I certainly didn't want anything else to happen to him, and since I began to see myself as the kiss of death anyhow I decided to be on the safe side and finally write him off the same as he had written me.

Our house was a big four-story Victorian eyesore with a wing slapped here and a porch stuck there and balconies and landings and traceries and weather vanes and from the very top of the stairs in the attic there was one little round window and from that window, if I stood on a chair, I could see all the way over to Lacey's, which meant that any time I wanted I could find my father on his beach chair, and from that little window, without his knowing it, I could watch him all day long if I wanted to as he'd greet old patients and hoodlums or bohemians from the poetry center who'd grab his hand or pat him on the shoulder as they went by. I'd watch him wave at a car that honked and then I'd watch him adjust his French beret and straighten his yellow ascot so he'd look his best because by now he had made a life for himself out on the sidewalk. His French beret, his ascot, his green and white striped beach chair with the Yellow Pages phone book under the leg with the shoe contraption had finally become as much a part of that corner as all the characters who hung around out there that Mr. Lacey cursed at and despised.

I remember the drunk who staggered up to him and tried to shove some money in his hand. I was smoking a cigarette and watching from the attic window one afternoon after school when I saw the drunk struggling with my father and for a minute (I pull out to pass an orange Mercedes-Benz) I thought they were in a fight so I was all ready to have to run over there when I realized that my father was actually motioning for the drunk to go away. Leave! Scadoo! Vamoose, my father was waving his good arm at the drunk, but the drunk wouldn't take no for an answer. Then I saw my father trying to reason with the drunk. First he pointed to the dead arm resting in his lap and then to the shoe contraption as he was tapping his breastbone with that quick bird look on his face to show the drunk what had happened, but the drunk, misunderstanding what my father was trying to say, wasn't going to be put off, not him! Oh no! He meant to give my father an honest well-meant handout even if it killed him so he started searching around until he found my father's pocket and then real fast, too fast for old Leo Fish, the drunk stuffed some money into it, elegantly tipped his hand to his forehead and as he staggered off my father's head dropped into his hand as he sat there devastated. When I told my mother the whole story I'm thinking as I'm getting back into the far right lane, all she did was shrug her shoulders a little as she flicked her head because, which I didn't know till then, my mother wasn't capable of feeling sad. Anger, yes, and rage without a doubt, but she didn't have a clue about what sadness was I'm thinking as the tears are welling up in my eyes but I did I'm thinking as I'm wiping my nose in my hand. "I'm so sorry," I whisper as I pass the exit for Danbury, Connecticut. *"Daddy!"* I'm whispering.

I *never meant to harm one hair on your head. Believe me and forgive me, please.*

But he didn't forgive me. Instead he sort of looked right through me from that time on, and then it happened, I remember, bad luck you could say, I got caught smoking in the girls' room by the music teacher and five minutes later I was back in the principal's office with the principal peering up over her glasses at me.

"Patricia," she begins. . . .

Okay! . . . It wasn't only the gray granite pallor of that whole miserable place. It was how rocklike it was and that nothing could ever dent it, not truth or reason or allowances for anything or kindness or lending a helping hand or a little goodwill, so this time I just sat there and looked at her while she went over all the rules. No smoking! No drinking! No cheating! Then back she went to stealing a story for an English composition class at the beginning of the year, which in her mind was never put to rest and she didn't mind telling me so. No, it wasn't my grades that presented any kind of problem she said. Obviously they were excellent. She wouldn't take that away from me, but there was something called "character" she said, and as far as she was concerned mine simply didn't measure up. That was the long and the short of it. I'd have to leave Vineland Senior High immediately, that day in fact. And since I didn't want to kill my father, as I was sitting in her office I began praying that by the time I got home from school that day the big dark man whom I once loved more than anyone on the face of the earth would be dead.

For myself, I'm remembering as the white Lincoln Continental full of all the Orientals passes me, there were only two things I was going to miss, the Raymond J. Thorpe Free Library, which was next to Vineland High, and a short little dumpy art teacher with an enormous bust, dyed black hair and chalk white skin who taught us everything from how to use eye makeup to what great literature would come to mean. Gladys Danzinger and her private seminars in the art room every Thursday after school on everything she thought was important, like how to bend like a lady, fix our hair, what to read, what music to listen to and proper nutrition. And she only held these seminars for the girls she had handpicked out of the entire class, girls she expected to "fire up" as she put it and make into something "very extra special" which were Janie Maxwell, Linda Alter, Emily Goode, me and Jessie Nobel because she said we were *the shining stars of the entire senior class*, so how could I tell her they kicked me out when I was already in her debt beyond anything I could ever even hope to repay. In fact, I'm remembering as I'm flying along, as our senior year progressed and she was getting more and more worked up about how fabulous we were, I would try harder and harder to avoid her whenever I could because in the first place, my debt to her was so great I could never begin to repay it and in the second, that look in her eyes of raw excitement was another terrible burden and frankly a little scary, too, so one day, without any explanation, I just stopped going to her house on Saturday mornings. I stopped going to her Thursday seminars in the art room after school and I started hiding out in the bathroom at lunch hour because I didn't feel like running into her in the hall or in the lunchroom and of course that was my Waterloo.

It all started with a little painting I did at the beginning of twelfth grade of a green woman sitting in a chair that didn't have any legs and that painting really excited Mrs. Danzinger. "Tell me, Patricia," she said, "why is the woman green and where are the legs of the chair," she whispered.

"Well," I said as I smiled nervously because by then I had met some pretty terrible teachers so I was trying to be careful because I didn't know what was coming next. Also, by then I had seen so much hideous cruelty inside a school room I wasn't sure what she was after. Was it a trick or a trap or did she mean to really give me an honest compliment? Then she grabbed me around my shoulders and clutched my left arm very tight as she started whispering something about being a "little river" that before her very eyes was beginning to inch out of its narrow little bed toward the "great unfathomable sea, a sea" she said, "that held the possibility of something greater than even *life*." She said that only a few can ever enter into this domain, she said it was a "vast and luminous space" and she said you could only find it through agonizing struggle but once you did, then she said you merged and became part of a "wondrous fullness."

And then she lowered her voice even more and tightened her squeeze on my arm even tighter as she whispered, "You, Peachy, are an *A R T I S T E!*"

Remember Rat? I'm thinking as I glance in the side-view mirror, pull out into the middle lane to pass a dark red station wagon with Florida plates, then pull back into the right-hand lane again, well, Leo Fish was her executioner. He was the one in the end who got her with the shovel. I watched him from the kitchen window three years before he had his stroke, flying around trying to swat at Rat with a shovel, that do-or-die look on his face, with his navy and red striped necktie flying over his shoulder. The trap he was setting had a piece of cheese and he had a poison sock he was going to stuff into her hole in the garage wall. She was a big gray thing with such fabulous dignity. She was a wonderful mother creature whom I had to see every day because she became like a person to me so I had to have a look at her almost the first thing when I got in from school. For months I used to leave her things to eat like scraps from the dinner table and sometimes Ginger Snaps and Oreos and whatever else I could find around the house. I thought about her all the time like early in the morning on my way to school because she was my good mother, not that Hendella wasn't good but with Hendella everything was always so dramatic and always such a big deal whereas with Rat, she had a simple easygoing way which made life peaceful and secure. She made things calm and in another way she was a lot like me because I'm the kind where two and two makes four, not nine hundred. We were both overly responsible and we didn't drink or curse and we didn't like things out of order or in disrepair and we both detested waste and excessiveness whereas with my mother it was like Pascal said, "One of those who prefers death to peace." With Hendella, two and two was twenty-five thousand because exaggeration was her middle name and exaggeration was always a little too close to lying for my two cents. With Hendella, the facts of any matter bored her out of her mind because Hendella lived in a world of her own invention whereas Rat was a real person like maybe she was a waitress at the Horn and Hardart Automat on Sixteenth Street in Philadelphia where her executioner, Leo Fish, used to take me to breakfast in the good old days when he'd have things like frizzled beef on toast, coffee and two doughnuts with all his hoodlum friends, those gorillas he used to hang around with whenever he had a minute with their wide lapels and their pointy navy blue suede shoes and their diamond rings and their gold ID bracelets and their money on the game or on the fight so I'd think about Rat because she was my Fairy Queen. She was my firm fat splendid creature who wore pearls and she always had glistening little dangles in her ears and a little feather boa around her shoulders and high-heel black patent-leather shoes. She had a mansion in the garage wall and I knew every inch of it and every piece of furniture, the stove, the pipes, her rocking chair, where she kept the cash (it was hidden in a coffee can under the piano).

"To Miss Eloise Boden" I wrote at the top of the page.

"In my new Okay Elementary School, the sixth-grade teacher's name is Mrs. Drummand-Rat," the story began. "A few of her intimates will call her Doris but that doesn't come so fast," I wrote, "oh no, that takes years, because that's the goal, to be worthy! Mrs. Drummand-Rat's job was to teach," I wrote. "Her job was to let all the little children know the truth. Notice, she's seven and a half feet tall and she's wearing a white silk dress with pearl buttons at the wrist that comes almost to her shoes and she has thick white hair that she wears in braided coils so it looks like a silver halo and she's wise! The All-Knowing One. And she's gentle, of course! But she can't let those little fourth graders know this," I wrote, "because if they find out they'll skin her alive. They'll suck the blood directly out of all her veins. Be nice to those little greedy monsters and just see what happens.

They'll take the chimney if they can get their hands on it—the front door—the icebox. I tell you they'll swipe her car if she turns her back on them for even a minute. It's the hubcaps, lady, that's what matters, the radio, the lighter! No more jokes about the human being because we've had enough! *Ha Ha Ha* Mrs. Drummand-Rat was laughing—No more of them fairy tales she's telling all the kids. Survival, she'll say! That's the whole entire purpose. To simply stay alive and outsmart all them executioners she's telling all the little children. During the war I was a vegetable cook behind the White House, she's telling them. Passed it every day on my way to work. It was when they jumped Pearl Harbor, what they call the Second World War, she's telling all the children who are sitting in front of her all milk-fed and formless with bright ribbons in their hair. But no, suddenly tears are in her eyes. No! Not to cry! Don't you do it, Mrs. Drummand-Rat! Instead tell them you'll give them As for toughing it out like you just were talking about. Come on! Tell them you'll give all of them As for *not* being so obedient and for *not* being so damn stinking polite, okay? You have to tell them that the truth is always a gift so they have to speak only *what's true* Mrs. Drummand-Rat, or else one day they'll go completely nuts and crazy. So come on," I wrote, "Don't back off! Don't be cowardly about it as Dorothy Jack stands up and brazenly pulls a gigantic boogie out of her nose as everybody begins to go wild . . .

They yell *bravissimo*.

They start whistling through two fingers. . . . Hoots and cat-calls are coming from all the children in my new Okay Elementary School because they love Dorothy Jack. She's ugly, but they love her anyhow. No sin to be ugly here. No crime. No sentence for life. See, they're throwing roses at her, coins, their shoes. All the little children are jumping up and down in their seats while they're banging their fists on the desks because she got such a fabulous boogie this time, a real prize, it's a doozie alright. . . .

I found Rat lying on her side over near the trash can. Her eyes were wide open and there was dried blood crusted all around her nostrils and in her ears and all around her mouth. Flies and maggots were swarming all over her as I rushed over and picked her up by her majestic tail.

A decent burial *please* I was begging Leo Fish. *Please* I was begging him. She was my Fairy Queen. She was a goddess, I was begging him as he was charging me like a bull. Then he knocked her out of my hand and grabbed me by the arm and started pulling me toward the kitchen so he could scrub my fingers where I was holding onto her as I started shouting, *Oh no you don't Leo Fish! there's no one who will absolve you for what you did to her like there's no one to absolve you either Eloise Boden for what you did to Alice Weinrot and to Dorothy Jack or to all of us who watched you teaching so much hideous cruelty."*

That's how it ended, the little story I was supposed to have stolen from Rudyard Kipling at the beginning of my senior year. And why was I so happy to write that story? Because how else was I going to hold onto all of it—to Rat and to old Leo Fish and to the way he smelled and to my mother's white silk blouse that had pearl buttons at the wrist and to the way she looked when she was young and to the way the world was then.

How else was I ever going to keep the house on Valley Avenue or the coal tar smell of the electric plant or how I felt when I looked at Eloise Boden's thin white hair that hid those other secret evil eyes because that was what I had! It was mine! *Mine! M i n e!* It belonged to me and what I wanted was to hold on to all of it forever so I wrote it down so how could they have ever come to Rudyard Kipling?

That's what I would like to know I'm shouting at the fog and at the dark and at the night that's beginning to mushroom up all around the green Cutlass station wagon as I pull over into the shoulder of the road, stop the car and finally let go the avalanche, the sobbing and the crying and the gasping for all that's gone and for all that never even had a chance.

"Life's too short to ever wear anything ugly."—*Loretta Fish*

Chapter

13

The living room of my brother Charlie's house glows gold in the light of all the candles. Cascades of white orchids tumble out of old porcelain tubs in front of the fireplace. Big bowls of white roses are on all the tables, and small potted trees are in all the corners of the room.

A young girl in a black miniskirt, thick white socks and white sneakers, with dyed jet-black hair that goes straight up and one enormous black-and-white plastic earring is serving caviar canapés before the ceremony begins. The smell of food mingles with the Victorian chairs and Oriental rugs and the big black hunks of modern sculpture that are everywhere. And as I look past all my aunts and great aunts with their spindly legs and children darting in white frilly dresses, my eyes fill as I catch the first glimpse of Suzie Fish standing by the fireplace in her antique wedding dress. As she sees us she comes flying over and grabs hold of me with one arm as her other arm clutches my mother and the three of us, Hendella, Suzie and I, cling to each other with tears streaming down our faces.

Then Loretta sees us and she comes flying over and we all stand huddled in the doorway holding onto each other with those same tears streaming down our faces.

As I wipe my eyes I see my mother's sister, Olivia Krantz sitting on the dark blue velvet sofa grinning at me in a red and tan checkered suit, white Nike sneakers, black fishnet stockings, a green wool scarf around her neck and a huge fake-fur turban next to her grown mongoloid daughter Olympia whom she used to dress up as the Easter Bunny for Halloween.

When I was little I used to watch Aunt Olivia stuff cotton into the spaces where some of her teeth were missing. She used to read palms and she claimed her late husband, Adolph, and Grandfather Heinfling would come over on "a regular basis" long after they were dead to tell her what stocks to buy. Sometimes she said they brought Beethoven along or sometimes Jimmy Dean or else sometimes she'd tell me they'd ask her to meet them at the Bird Sanctuary right off of Route 555 and she'd say, "I'll be there, of course! Immediately!" so as not to give them the impression of being rude. As I bend to kiss her, suddenly I long for all the letters she used to write to me when I was young, and for her notepaper that had a picture of the Cathedral of Notre Dame, and for her flowery swirling signature that went up a little hand-drawn bar of music with each note one of the letters of her name. She lived in a little house in Newfield with my cousin Olympia and as I'm hugging her I'm remembering how all the houses on that block used to remind

me of a string of white men's shirts hanging sadly on a clothes-
line in the sun. Whenever my mother took me over there, Aunt
"Livie" would take me up to her bedroom and then we'd go
through all her bureau drawers and then through her closets
and then through her old steamer trunk because she liked to
show off certain items—a ticket stub, a certain button, an old
fur sling with two glass eyes that had little black silk feet. Then
she'd show me the blue eyelet dress she wore the day she sailed
for France with my grandmother and my grandfather. Aunt
Livie reminded me of cobwebs. She was skinny with a long
neck and fragile hands and that big Heinfling schnoz and a lot
of sentiment. She was all dreamy crystal ball predictions about
mysterious ports with dark lovers for me she'd say as she gazed
at my palm. "Ah," she'd whisper so Hendella wouldn't hear,
"such nights of passion my darling. *Ooh la la!*" she'd croon in the
closed-in sun porch of that little house in Newfield where she
lived inside her huge collection of small glass animals that were
displayed on thin glass shelves inside all the windows. Aunt
Livie loved me fiercely but she was a terrible burden to me then.
Then she was a weird creature I was afraid to get too close to.
But now as she grabs my hand, kisses it and then holds it next to
her cheek as she's smiling wildly at me, she makes me long for
the house in Newfield and for all those letters and for her
flowery swirling signature because it's *mine!* This is what I have
like I have Hendella and Ruthie and Suzie Fish and my cousin
Olympia Krantz with her straight sand-colored hair and her
small thick eyes and pug nose and round face with its vague
indiscernible cast who stood kicking the grass in her big navy

dirndl and big black patent Mary Janes the day we laid my grandfather in the ground beside his son Monroe in the little cemetery across from the state mental hospital, this old little girl sitting next to her mother who doesn't know if she's a bird or a song or a poem or what, all she knows is that her mother will always be there to wipe her nose and put the ribbon back in her hair as she wanders through her deathless dream that has no time or seasons. For my cousin Olympia Krantz love and sorrow don't get all jumbled so that half the time she doesn't know which is which. For her there's no dread of loss so great that she starts breathing heavy when she sees her family sitting bravely in a dark blue velvet sofa, all of them a stone's throw away from the end. For her, no judging them for what they did or didn't do when she was a child and then in the end deciding it didn't matter anyhow because they loved her and they were human which means they did the best they knew how I'm thinking as I hug Olympia, kiss her, hug her and then kiss her again.

Uncle Archie's hair has gotten completely white. He stands up as we come over. He's the fatalist, the sad heir to the whole chicken and egg empire now that his brother Monroe is gone. Uncle Archie wears a beeper on his belt so his neighbors can let him know at a moment's notice if someone's trying to steal his patio furniture. When I was little he used to tell me that his father's voice could make him vomit from fear and that sometimes he'd hide in the broom closet all day long for fear of my grandfather's rages, but those stories would fly off his back like dust. They didn't seem to come from where any feelings were.

Nothing did with him. Nothing ever made even the smallest dent on Archie's constant smile, his soft easy laugh and the sweet slap I'd get as he tweaked the tip of my nose. Weddings didn't phase him and neither did funerals, or even buying the coffin for my baby, because this was Uncle Archie's job, this was what he had to do and he always measured up except with Uncle Archie, you never knew what he was thinking because he never had much to say.

Like you never knew what Aunt Hilda was thinking for that matter either, I'm thinking, as Aunt Hilda comes over to carefully ask why Ruthie isn't here as she's taking a thread off my sleeve. Everything with them was always a big secret I'm thinking as I hug Aunt Hilda. It was such a big secret which synagogue they joined after they decided to leave Rabbi Massengil because of "that sordid business with the television set," to quote Aunt Hilda word for word. It became a big secret where they went in the winter for their two week vacation—was it West Palm Beach or was it Key West? No one knew and they wouldn't let on to anyone like they wouldn't let on about who their new dentist was after they moved out of East Vineland or where they got their baby grand or any information about their daughter Georgia's husband. No one knew a thing about him or what he did or where he went to school and no one was invited to the wedding either. All they'd ever say was that business was terrible so they had to hold on to every cent they could get their hands on because they got stuck with a lemon as far as the chicken and egg industry was concerned. No little luxuries like a new fur coat or a little pair of diamond studs in years, they'd say as they'd shoot each other looks because business was still bad they'd tell everybody.

But everybody knew the truth was that long ago Uncle Archie got very sick, only no one knew what he had or who was treating him since he stopped using my father. We all knew Uncle Archie and Aunt Hilda found a few big fancy specialists up in Philadelphia but no names were ever mentioned and there was nothing but halves of stories told to everyone all the way back to Leo Fish who had been Uncle Archie's own personal slave night and day from the day he came into the family and then suddenly when Uncle Archie stopped calling him every other minute to complain about everything from an ingrown toenail to Aunt Hilda's gallbladder attack my father went completely off his rocker.

"Years of free medical attention for the whole rotten family wasn't good enough," he seethed. "Oh *no!* For every pimple," my father yelled as all the veins in his neck popped out, "for every bellyache, for every little itch and rash and touch of indigestion Archie Heinfling thought nothing whatsoever of calling me at two or three in the morning with never a gift or a smile or a single word of appreciation in all these years and why? because Archie Heinfling thought it was all *just coming to him, didn't he?* Well, we'll see what's coming to him," my father raged, because from the moment he heard about the "specialists" from Philadelphia all hell broke loose.

"What *pigs!*" he shouted. "What chiseling, no-good, two-timing *bums!* What disgusting freeloading sons of *bitches* those two are! She's a stinking little sneak who whispers 'hello' behind her hand like it's some kind of confidential information and

Archie Heinfling—What a two-faced, no-good, lousy, scheming coward who could two-time his own brother-in-law without so much as batting an *eye*. A new doctor?" he seethed, "a fancy *'specialist'*?" Every time he thought of it, it made my father want to kill Uncle Archie and Aunt Hilda and he'd be glad to throw in little Granny Heinfling for that matter, too.

After that, whenever Leo Fish saw my grandmother and grandfather on Landis Avenue waiting for a cab to come to our house for dinner, he wouldn't pick them up. He just kept driving. When they walked in the door he slipped out the back, locked himself in his office and turned on the game. He stopped going there for holidays and for Friday night dinners and for lunch on Sunday afternoons and when he had to speak to them it was with pure ice and rage. It was never the same again. Not even nearly. Then one night, the fatal night, at our house at the dinner table my grandmother, who barely tread when she walked (the little elf picked her way through life peering in every direction in her little clear plastic glasses always so careful not to hurt a flea), Dare she ask him about a rash that popped up between her fingers?

Yes, and with that the ball game was all over. Ninth inning. Two outs with the bases loaded and Flossie Cohen Heinfling sinks a fly into deep left field.

"Ah *ha!*" my father smoldered as he leapt up from his chair at the dinner table. "Not good enough for your son *the Archibald Felix Heinfling anymore! Oh no! Only good enough for some free advice at the dinner table about a rash?*" he seethed as he peered at my grandmother.

"Your Mother, Hendella," he shouted, "this noodge over here, is some real cockamamie *lulu!* She's a real little hipper-dipper—this one," he yelled as he threw down his napkin, and then it was as if the entire State of New Jersey had just blown up. Nothing was left—Oceans, rivers, malls and highways were all smashed. Nothing was spared in the avalanche that began with his accusing my grandmother of every treachery under the sun. For a bursa she dared consult an orthopedic surgeon after he told her precisely what the trouble was. A vaginal itch she dared consult one of her grandniece's husbands about because he was some cockamamie gynecologist but since he was from *New York City,* "that made him a Big *Fancy Deal,*" he was shouting. For every illness anyone in the family ever discussed with anyone but him he was on the rampage. Never mind the way he stopped working for three full months to care for Uncle Monroe with never a single word of thanks from anybody, and never mind all the nights he sat up with "Pappa" and his rotten nervous stomach and his gas and his attacks of diarrhea. For every false alarm, for every scratch, for every belch or hiccup, they didn't mind bothering him till he went loonie. Who did they think they were? That's what he would like to know he was raging at little Flossie Heinfling who sat cowering as Charlie and I slipped straight down from our dining room chairs onto the rug, crawled on all fours under the table to the edge of the dining room and then ran like hell for the stairs.

All night we heard Hendella and Leo Fish screaming at each other. We heard doors slamming. We heard water flushing. On nights like that I had to play with myself for hours in order to get any sleep at all. Their fights stayed with me for days. They hung around the house like a dye that colored everything I'm thinking, as Rabbi Julian Massengil is going up to the fireplace and as he raises his arms to quiet everyone, as a hush falls over the living room, as everyone becomes still with expectancy, I feel two arms come around my shoulders from behind as a face comes into my neck, and as I feel the kiss I also feel the soft hair on my neck and as I turn I see the bright apple smile, the big white teeth and the wide brown eyes of a face that for an instant makes me think I'm looking at myself, and then, a split second of confusion, and then the pure unspeakable joy of realizing that it's not me I'm looking at but Ruthie.

And as we're hugging with our faces pressed against each other's and then as we start swaying as we keep hugging and smiling, I hear my mother telling someone "Take my daughter, Peachy." I hear her whisper, "No confidence in herself at all," she's whispering in her muffled highly-confidential tone of voice. "Never mind the fact that Peachy has *everything!*" she whispers. "Beauty! Intelligence! Breeding! Style! You name it, she's got it. But so *quiet!* My goodness! She's another Harpo Marx," I hear my mother whisper. "And please! Don't ask me why she never says two words to anyone. It's a real mystery to me I can assure you because it certainly doesn't have anything to do with her upbringing, I can vouch for that. She was *the* apple of her father's eye. My *God!*" she's whispering. "Anything that child wanted her father *lavished* on her, cashmere sweaters! a Schwinn bike! cultured pearls! A three-quarter length beaver coat when she was barely seventeen years old, but did she ever once give her father even one whole sentence in her life? Did she ever give *anyone* even one whole sentence in her life with the exception of my brother Archie?" she whispers. "But if you ask me, the real reason she lacks the self-confidence to speak out is simply because she married that jerk before she was even out of *high school!* She ran off with that Alfred Marvel when she was still too young to even tie her shoelaces. The boy was someone her father and I were less than thrilled about if you know what I mean. Oh sure," I hear her whispering, "he was a nice boy and he came from a half-decent family or so we thought at the time, but when push came to shove, very sick! And I mean in the head, so of course how could she develop? How could she discover what she was all about or that she even had a voice," she's whispering while at the same time the Rabbi is raising his arms to the assembled guests, "Dear friends, we are gathered today to join in holy matrimony this man and this woman," Rabbi Massengil's melodious voice is crooning. "Dear Susan and Arthur," he's saying, his arms raised so high that the full sleeves of his robe billow out like the masts of some black sailing ship of death, "God has blessed the two of you," he says, "with the greatest gift bestowed to humankind. But!" he says, "in the name of this great love you will be called upon to make enormous sacrifices! Don't shrink from this because Love Means Sacrifice! So make your Sacrifice an exalted privilege.

"Dear Arthur and Susan, I implore you!" he's saying, as Ruthie, my mother, me and whomever my mother's talking to are squashing ourselves into the blue velvet sofa, and as we're all trying to get comfortable, as I adjust my legs and then get my

back straight so I can finally settle down and savor the ceremony I hear my mother whispering, "It was sex and sex alone
that drove me like there was a secret propeller somewhere deep
inside my body that was always purring. When I was young,"
she's whispering, "I found myself gaping at grown women, their
breasts, their legs and that dark mysterious center they had that
drove men wild and I used to think—Some day I too will be a
woman! Which to me that meant only one thing—*sex!!*" I hear
her whispering. "For me *sex* was the thrilling light at the end of
every tunnel. Sex was the wonder and the curiosity and *the
Excitement of Excitements.* And then one day that first red drop
of blood that heralded the coming of my time," I hear her
whispering. "And now," I hear her whispering, "the slow steady
loss of power that winds you up a babbling old bat without teeth
or hair, not even on your *pussy!*" I hear her whispering. "Three
are left," I hear her whispering, "just like a catfish's chin.

"Tell me," I hear her whispering, "what did you say your name
is? Sensacapelli? I see," she whispers, "and what do you do, Mr.
Sensacapelli? Oh! A *neurosurgeon!*" I hear her whispering. "I
see," I hear her say. "And your wife?" I hear her whisper. "I see," I
hear her say. "Well," I hear her say, "I know a very lovely young
woman who just so happens to be here tonight but before I
point her out to you, let me ask you this, Do you love your
mother? Do you love your father? Do you Italians love your
parents and venerate them the way we Jewish people do?
Because this lovely young woman I want to introduce just so
happens to be my own extraordinary, charming, beautiful and
intelligent daughter who loves her mother like I loved my

mother. I don't know why the children love me as much as they do," she says, "because sometimes maybe I talk a little bit too much, everybody tells me that, but she still loves me anyhow, don't ask me why," I hear her whispering.

And then I hear her chuckling as Rabbi Massengil is beginning to describe to Susan and Arthur the meaning of a Jewish home. "Did you know that this Rabbi Julian Massengil is absolutely *crazy!*" I hear Hendella whispering. "Do you know that he's a real first-class *lunatic!* Let me tell you that if it wasn't for my son Charlie Fish they would have run that nut out of town a long time ago. Why? You want to know *why.* . . . Because of that whole television set scandal!" I hear her whispering. "You mean you don't know?" I hear her whispering. "You didn't hear what that lunatic had the temerity to pull on the entire congregation? Well, three years ago, and on *Rosh Hashana* no less, during the sermon that the rabbi always delivers every Rosh Hashana which is the most important sermon of the entire year, that nut had the nerve to tell the entire congregation of Beth Or that we are not only living in the Messianic Era, he dares to say, *But!* he says, we should be happy to know that the *Messiah is in Beth Or as he is speaking!* And with that that nut up there—that lunatic Rabbi Julian Massengil—goes over to the Ark, presses the button, the golden doors open up as usual and what do you think is right there before our very eyes? *In front of all the Holy Scrolls of our sacred Talmud!* Right in the very center inside the doors? What do you think the entire congregation was suddenly looking at? You'll never guess," I hear her whispering, "not if you live to be a thousand years old, you'll never guess what we were staring at with all our mouths wide *open!* It was a *twenty-seven-inch Sony television set* with, get this," she whispers, "a *holy tallis over it* right there inside the Ark *in front of the ten books of Moses!* And that's not all," she whispers. "The next thing, the little assistant rabbi, Rabbi Barry Trachenberg, comes forward, and together they carry the television set with, mind you, the blue and white tallis over it up to the pulpit where he dares to say to everybody in the synagogue that they are now looking at *The Messiah.*

"'My most dearly beloved congregation of Beth Or,' he says, *'This, I want you all to know is The Messiah!*

"'TELEVISION!' he starts screaming like he's lost his mind. 'This!' he starts shouting while his hands are flying all around. 'This!' he's screaming, 'is what brought *peace to Vietnam! This!'* he says, as he bends to kiss it, 'is the potential for *compassion, growth* and *understanding.* Think of it,' he began to shout, 'if television cameras and a crew of committed newspeople could have gotten into the camps, into Treblinka, into Bergen-Belsen and into Auschwitz in time, millions upon millions of lives would have been *SAVED!'* he was yelling as some of the members of the congregation began getting up and actually walking out of there but did that stop him? No, it did NOT," I hear her whispering. "Not only did it *not* stop him, it looked to me like it fired him up even more because next thing he went into a long harangue about all the places TV had gone and there was peace after that instead of hatred, disharmony and bloodshed. But by then three quarters of the congregation had left the synagogue in a fury including yours truly, because I say 'good riddance to bad rubbish,'" I hear her whispering, "because who was Julian Massengil to decide all by himself who *is* and who is *not* the Messiah or if a twenty-seven-inch Sony television set *is* or is *not* the Messiah. Don't they have to take a vote?

"Anyhow, my son, Charlie Fish, thinks Julian Massengil is a *genius!* That's right, Dr. Sensacapelli, even though half of Vineland doesn't speak to the rabbi anymore, Charlie does, and he insists that I do, too, so of course I do because frankly who gives a damn, and anyhow why make a fuss. But between you and me I think he's a nut," she's whispering to this Dr. Sensacapelli, whom I have to get a glimpse of I'm thinking as I'm fishing around in my pocketbook for my compact to use like a little periscope so I can see the poor devil she's got snared in her net this time, the latest victim of her mega-mouth weapon that she's been firing away at nonstop since the moment she's laid eyes on him.

"Did you know or did you ever hear of my late husband, Leo Fish?" I hear her whispering in hushed tones as I flick my compact mirror around slowly until it finally catches his reflection—*Hm-m-m-m* I'm thinking, not bad! He's dark and bald with a squared-off head, thick neck and thick broad shoulders. Elegant in a kind of gangster way, extremely sexy I'm thinking. Big nose which of course means he has a big you-know-what, that's what they say, I'm thinking. Soft brown eyes a lot like Leo Fish's which makes me feel instantly a little sad, and *m-m-m-m,* I like his hands. Very graceful dancing hands. They look like two great water creatures or like his hands are performers in a beautiful hand ballet and *what's more, the man is completely spellbound by Hendella!* His eyes are riveted to her face like two magnets while he's hanging onto every word she's uttering like he's in a *trance!*

"What a father! What a husband! What a surgeon!" I hear her whispering, "not to mention what a son-in-law he was to my father S.J. Heinfling *of East Vineland New Jersey.* Ah," she says, "how he gave and gave and gave to my whole family and with so much gentle love and kindness and compassion. But," she says, "the apple of his eye, in fact I might say the loves of his whole life were his daughter, Peachy, and his son Charlie Fish who in spite of the fact that he still worships that nutty, meshuganah rabbi who may I tell you everyone says enshrines his own television set at home in an Ark with its own private tallis in front of his own private Torah scrolls, but except for that one little flaw in my son he is like his father who was a *saint!*"

I see through my compact mirror that Dr. Sensacapelli is smiling and nodding his head in appreciation of every word that's coming out of her mouth. "Let me tell you," I hear her whispering under her breath, "as far as Leo Fish was concerned, *nothing* was too good for the children and I mean *nothing* and what's more, he had time for all their little needs and concerns and more than that he was fair and patient and *so sympathetic* it could break your heart. And what a gentleman, and what a dancer on top of that, especially the rumba. Naturally he had the opportunity of going into the chicken and egg business," she's whispering in hot, hushed tones. "My father offered him a very fine position with the company. But no," she whispers as Susan and Arthur are putting the rings carefully on each other's fingers, "my Leo could never have worked in a chicken coop, *God forbid!* Not with all that chicken shit they had in there and the *stink!* Oh my GOD! that *ammonia* smell could kill a *horse!*

"You couldn't breathe inside those damn sticking coops for even a minute," she's whispering, "but stink or no stink," I hear her saying, "we were *dethroned royalty!* Yes! that's right! That's *exactly what we were!* My father's home in East Vineland was swarming every week with luminaries from the sports world and from the art world and from the world of *business and commerce!* My *God!* I never saw my mother peel a potato in my whole *life!* Mama used to always say she couldn't wait for the day when she'd be down to only one maid and let me tell you Mama had more diamonds on one hand," she's whispering, "than anyone in Vineland had on two, not that she wore them every minute like some of those women, but take my word, we lived on bran- dished gold and woven tapestries.

"Come *on!*" she's whispering, "we drank out of gold and ruby goblets every single night of the week and ate dinner every night with nothing but solid gold forks and knives that each weighed a *ton* and our coffee was poured by our houseman Stanhope Stinger from an exquisite silver pitcher into only the finest bone china cups from Lenox Massachusetts. And may I tell you, Dr. Sensacapelli, the walls of our dining room had a hand-painted mural of naked sea nymphs dancing in a circle done by Elliot Kretchner who was a very famous artist in his day because that was the way my father insisted on *everything!* His grass! His flower garden! His gazebo out back. *Please!* Not to mention the fact that we never had to think twice about what we spent or what we gave a maid or what we would simply throw down the toilet if we felt like it," she whispers as Suzie and Arthur are bowing their heads for the closing benediction.

"And on top of that, as if all that wasn't *enough*, I was engaged to a *physician! No chicken shit all over my shoes for the rest of my life! No siree!*

"*I was getting out*," she's whispering as the rabbi raises his long frail hands high in the air.

"And now," he says, "by the powers vested in me by the State of New Jersey and by the laws of the State of Israel I now pronounce you Arthur, and you Susan, man and wife!"

And as Arthur is crashing down his heel on the wineglass on the floor in front of him, as he grabs Suzie and holds her and kisses her lips, as they turn from the rabbi, their faces radiant with so much happiness, my eye, for some unknowable reason travels to the left and then to the front door in the hall at the exact instant that it opens and Alfred Marvel walks in, late of course, with a young muscular woman in a red suit, pitch black hair and a little red hat on her head with a red matching veil.

"Luck is God."—*Rabbi Julian Massengil*

Chapter

14

So there you are, finally, I'm thinking, my good old bear whom I've been waiting for so very long in this odd place where nothing much seemed to have happened except the waiting. Come up, you say, to where the parts don't squeak and all my hair falls loose across a piece of sunshine. Take me with you, my good old turtle, for so long I've been sitting on hard shells that crack and break and fall away like all the bad worst dreams of losing teeth and wiggly ones because nothing was ever here or there except the waiting and yet no time at all, like it was only yesterday. So strange this whole time thing, like it must not go from south to north and then shoot straight ahead like it feels it does. I think it piles up in stacks and then those stacks must all get piled up on other stacks and this stacking business must go on and on and on forever in your head I'm thinking as I'm gazing at his expensive charcoal pinstripe suit from Mr. Portante who charges eighteen hundred dollars for just the jacket alone, not to mention the crocodile shoes and the Hermès necktie and his best blue shirt from Ascot Chang.

I look over at the girlfriend—young and so beautiful and so full of confidence like some kind of sexual warrior—and then as I look down at my own plain black suit with my dingy gray satin blouse, certainly nothing like he has on or what his girlfriend's wearing. I'm beginning to feel a little on the drab side like I could have done a whole lot better as far as fashion goes but then let's face it, fashionwise I've never known how to do any better anyhow and I never will. I don't know what to do with scarves, my skirts are always too long, my blouses are plain and my shoes are always a little too much on the sensible side I'm thinking as Hendella, Ruthie and I are struggling to get up out of the dark blue velvet couch.

Marriage really throws you, especially when you get married too young. It just completely throws you I'm thinking as we're finally up on our feet again.

And as we slowly begin threading our way through the pack of friends and relatives toward the dining room I bend over and whisper into my mother's ear, "Tell me Hendella," I say, "what one thing does a person need to have in order to get through in this life? I mean, what do Ruthie and I really need in order to survive?" I ask my mother in a hushed tone of voice as we start moving toward the buffet.

"Take your time," I whisper. "Think carefully about what I'm asking," I whisper to her.

But without pausing a second to even catch her breath she

whispers back as though she's been thinking about how to answer this very question all her life, "A *husband, dummy!* Come *on!*" she says as she shoots me a fierce and filthy look. "A *husband!*" she says as I'm fishing out my compact again so I can keep track of Alfred through the round mirror on top of the flat little cake of pressed face power as he goes over to the fireplace, kisses Suzie Fish, hugs her and then kisses her again.

"A *husband!*" my mother's whispering as we keep moving toward the lavish buffet where a whole shimmering poached salmon in a thin dill sauce, golden crisp fried chicken, a huge cut-crystal punch bowl brimming to the top with iced pink jumbo shrimp, an enormous silver tray filled with spaghetti and meatballs, a large wooden bowl filled with a crisp green salad, little knots and swirls of homemade rolls, a low silver tray filled with a sweet potato casserole that has burnt marshmallows melted into a thick crust on the top, a turkey, a ham that has chunks of cranberry sauce inside thick yellow pineapple rings and little cannolis made of eggplants that are nestling in a heavy marinara. "Did you hear what I said? I said every woman under the sun needs a *husband.* You! Ruthie and *Everyone! Because my dear, a woman is nothing without a man!*" she's whispering as I'm twisting my compact mirror lower now so I can catch a glimpse of his girlfriend's legs. Oh my *God!* I'm thinking, she'll kill him with legs like that! With his knees he should never jog with anyone that young! Alfred! I whisper into my compact mirror, there's no fool like an old fool, so you better ask yourself before you marry her, Does this girl truly care about me? Would this girl trace my flat feet onto a piece of onionskin paper and then rush the tracings over to the orthopedic supply house the way Peachy did, so they could make you up a pair of orthotics before we went to Atlantic City for the summer? I'm remembering as we keep moving forward slowly toward the huge crystal punch bowl filled with the iced pink jumbo shrimp which is at the beginning of the whole lavish food extravaganza. Of course she wouldn't, I whisper to his reflection in the center of my compact mirror because how could you get that kind of kindness and understanding from a person who can't even spell the word arthritis let alone have any pity for it or for your poor knees or for your poor flat pronated feet I'm whispering as an oldish-looking woman comes up to me, puts out her hand and stares me dead in the eye.

And as my eyes are torn away from the reflection of Alfred in my compact mirror and my brow wrinkles for those few moments that recognition takes, as I look into this woman's eyes hidden in the folds of skin between the eyebrows and the bags underneath the eyelid, is Annie Weiss.

"Peachy Fish!" she says.

"Oh my *God!*" I'm thinking as I gaze at the face in front of me. Never in ten million years would I have recognized this person. Every trace of her youthfulness, every hint of that special spirit she once had is completely gone. This person standing in front of me, this shadow of someone who was the first great love of my life is an old ugly bag . . . the same as I must be to her.

My God, I'm thinking, as I feel myself somehow suddenly cut off and separate from everyone in the room as though I'm tumbling through space. It's like being trapped for a moment in a vise that combines the past, the present, hope and defeat in one flash that has always been and that shall always continue forever I'm thinking as I reach out and take her hand and look at her.

"Let's go out on the sun porch where we can talk!" she says as I stare at this wizened little skinny shell, this drab middle-aged hag who looks more like some of my friends' mothers than a friend of my own with her dyed blond hair with its tight permanent frizz, her skinny hollow body and her dark miserable dress.

And as we turn away from the buffet table and begin walking, I feel again the Vineland train station woods in the early fall when the creek looked like an opal that still held the whole golden summer in it . . . I feel the sun streaming through the open places in the trees in great bands of smoky gold and most of all I remember those waves that never came again—never, never, never, never, never. . . .

Their governess who never stopped talking and chain-smoked all the time told us that little girls were dirty buckets who had to scrub their vizzies with a rag to get the stink away. What stink? we'd ask. The stink! *The stink!* she'd yell. Or else she'd tell us she had a terrible urge to eat our fingers and maybe our toes too while she picked under Annie's nails with an orange stick to get them clean while we sat on white canvas lawn chairs under a tree wondering why flowers were never black which we decided must have had something to do with bees and what attracted them which always made us think there was something all worked out all around us all the time that had to do with everything including flowers and bees, some big mysterious something that was everywhere and it knew everything. We decided red flowers were crazy except not roses, but poppies screamed like her mother when she yelled at their cook and that I was afraid of the color blue because it reminded me of grandfather Heinfling's eyes.

In the woods behind the Vineland train station she asked me once to look inside her vizzy and tell her exactly what I saw because she said she couldn't see in there except with a mirror and she said that one mirror never gave an accurate picture anyhow because she said if you really want to know what something looks like you have to use two mirrors because the first mirror creates a distortion that the second mirror completely reverses. So of course I looked in there because I wanted her to be my best friend and while I was looking she told me how she once saw her parents doing it. She said she pretended to be asleep on the sofa in their bedroom and she said they never bothered to kick her out and then she said that if I lay very still she'd show me how they did it. So of course I lay very still because I wanted her to be my best friend and then she rolled on top of me in all that soft brown spongy earth that was covered over with a blanket of thick brown pine needles and as she started rocking she started kissing me on the lips which I didn't like but I let her do it anyhow while she started rocking to show me how her parents did it and as she did her little cotton underpants got soaking wet from all the sweat as her little bone kept rubbing around down there while she was telling me about a boy who lived behind her who always went around his room with nothing on. Then she said that if I wanted I could come over and we could watch him through her father's binoculars and as she kept rocking I could look right in her mouth because it was so close to mine with her dark hair touching my cheek and her warm breath while she kept rocking and rocking and rocking and rocking and then it happened—*bam!* all over my face and down my legs and in my toes and in my fingers, waves and waves and waves of ecstacy coming all over me again and again and again and again and again. . . .

She went to Miss Crawford's which was a school for little debutante types who all wore plaid kilts and yellow Shetland sweaters while my school was a big Gothic monster right in the middle of Route 555 next to the Ivy Mount Cemetery where we used to eat lunch on nice days, while right across the road Miss Crawford's gleamed like a jewel with its glass walls and sleek blue overhanging roof and grand sprawling lawn that rolled off into all the trees and shrubbery that bordered it. She lived in a red brick mansion on Valley Avenue that had a huge library that had the whole zodiac in the ceiling and it had a black-and-white marble floor in the dining room and there were three living rooms that all had black-and-white marble floors with mirrors everywhere and big crystal chandeliers that had dangling rock amethysts that looked, when the lights were on, like a whole glittering little universe strung up to an immense wrought-iron galaxy and every time I went over there the smell of Lysol brand disinfectant came up to hit me the first thing and forever more the smell of Lysol brand disinfectant became for me the smell of wealth, opulence and having made it in the world.

Her mother was a fat soprano with dyed-black hair who

squashed herself into low-cut glittering evening dresses and she wore huge hats with feathers and veils and sequins and in every room including Annie's bedroom a portrait of "Aunt Lilly" smiled down at you along with all the busts in iron and bronze and plaster on almost every table in that house so that every time you looked around there she was one way or another with her coiffed metal hair and her frozen metal grin in that Lysol-smelling world that had pink marble sinks with gold swans for the hot and cold, and gold falcons in the bathtubs, and gray carpets everywhere, even inside the closets.

But most of all it was Annie's father, "Uncle Horace," with his big bay window belly who scared the daylights out of me. As many times as I ever saw him he never nodded hello to me until the night that Annie told me he wanted to show us his thing for educational purposes. I was dumbfounded. But then when I saw Uncle Horace in a yellow satin bath robe coming toward me whispering that he was a prisoner, he said, of every client in his law firm, a prisoner, he was huffing, of every party Aunt Lilly ever threw, a prisoner, he mumbled as he began untying the sash, of every member of the board of directors of Rutgers University, I ran—Did I *run!* Out of their house and across the park and over the lawn of the School for Feeble-Minded Girls and then up over Landis Avenue like a pack of wild wolves were at my tail.

We used to take turns tickling and scratching each other's arms in the movies and on the train or on the bus. We used to tickle and scratch each other's hands and each other's necks in Sunday school and in the Vineland train station woods on

Saturdays, sometimes we'd lie in the pine needles all day long back near where the hollowed-out logs had yellow toadstools growing in them and we'd tickle and scratch each other.

She had a little gold bracelet that she always wore which was a little chain with a gold heart dangling down near the catch and one Sunday afternoon I snatched it off her bathroom sink when she was in the shower and put it in my pocket.

Annie was the youngest of four daughters who all sang and took tap-dancing lessons and played the piano and spoke French as well as they spoke English and so with her little bracelet in my pocket some little bit of all that glamour and opulence belonged to me. Now it was as if I too had one little drop of all their gorgeous silverware and fabulous china plates and even a little piece of Aunt Lilly herself not to mention a bit of each of her sisters with some of their clothes thrown in. There were so many shoes and evening gowns and pocketbooks and dresses and skirts and jackets hanging next to each other in all their closets that I was floored. Their drawers were crammed with so many cashmere sweaters and satin slips and lacy night-gowns and real silk underwear and only the best of everything, the best schools, the best camps, the best cars, the best rugs, the best paintings, the best clothes. They had a butler and a chauffeur and a cook and two maids like a whole other popula-tion was always running around in there.

Her oldest sister Barbara had pink satin falsies that had little pink rosebuds for the nipples and we'd take turns stuffing them into our undershirts and then we'd fall on the floor in gales of laughter. All the other sisters had to turn themselves inside out just to get a smile out of fat old Uncle Horace with his big bay window belly and Aunt Lilly with her black patent-leather hair while all Barbara ever had to do was breathe. She had long black hair and green slanty eyes like a cat's and a long narrow body with an exquisite fragility about her like all she was a little satin thread, this beautiful accident of pure good luck whom everybody adored for no reason except that she was so extremely beautiful. And so, with Annie's little gold bracelet tucked safely in my pocket, one drop of Barbara's ravishing beauty belonged to me now too. But at lunch the day I stole the bracelet—and not because I wanted the bracelet but because I wanted the whole Weiss family—when Uncle Horace, who came to lunch that afternoon with his fly wide open so that anyone who looked could see his business, passed the butter to me, I felt his eyes glaring at me from the other side of the butter plate that he held a minute too long like his eyes were coals that were burning into me.

And as I felt him staring straight into my eyes I broke out in a sweat.

I began to tremble as I took the butter plate from him because his eyes kept staring at me without blinking and with Annie's gold bracelet clutched tightly in my fist the room began to spin and then, as I felt the blood draining from my face I began to feel a little clammy as I went limp, smelling as I went down that heavy smell of Lysol brand disinfectant drifting over from the marble mantle and up from the windowsills and baseboards that went all around the marble floor—that smell that to me became the acerbic smell of money, it became the arid smell of an invulnerability and of an invincible quality that broke the soul.

And then in August, right before school began, the Weiss family moved to San Francisco and with them went everything—the train station woods in autumn and the creek and the trees with the sunlight streaming through the branches as I walked around Vineland in a daze.

Once, when I was very young, I saw my mother going down the icy steps in front of my grandfather Heinfling's house. I was looking out the window watching as she was hanging onto the iron railing with both her hands, those hands that I used to stare at when I was little wondering every time I looked at them what they knew—what they touched—what they did in the dark with a man but as I watched her holding on to the railing that day her hands showed me something I had never seen before . . . Terror, which I began to understand as I was watching her and, as I watched her, for the first time the idea of death began to dawn on me and after that everything was different.

After that, I began to see the thin trees along the side of the chicken coops suddenly looking sad. A piece of cake with a bite taken out of it was sad. I saw something sad in my grandfather's dog sleeping in the sun. After that I saw sadness in a window shade that was halfway up or in a lamp that was lit in the day or in the old ratty piece of lace on the table in the hall that had a tear in it but after Annie moved away, instead of seeing the sadness here and there in certain things, I saw it in everything all the time. After she moved, the train station became unbearable, a completely desolate platform a second after it had been crammed with people made me feel like I was going to choke from something that was suddenly knotting up in my chest and as the train came tearing down the tracks half the time I didn't know whether to get on it or to jump in front of it. Almost every day I'd go over to the Weiss's red brick mansion on Valley Avenue and look at where all the living rooms were and where the dining room was and where the library was that had the whole zodiac in the ceiling, only now there were different people there with different cars in the garage and different porch furniture.

Every morning I took the bus to school the same as usual and every day I trudged those same musty halls only now I was numb and in a daze. It was the first loss I had ever had. It was the first hole that was ever drilled into me that diminished me in a way that I never really recovered from and ever so slightly from that day on I was changed.

On rainy days I'd cut school and go to the movies, on good days I ate my lunch in the cemetery even when it was too cold outside but that way at least I could look across the road and see Miss Crawford's even though I never went over there again like I never went back to the train station woods. Not ever. It was done, that feeling of being part of the earth that was ecstasy. . . .

"So what are you up to these days?" she's saying.

"Me?" I say, as I come out of my daze and stare at Annie Weiss. "Well, I'm raising my daughter and taking care of my mother who's getting old," I say as I point both of them out to her. "And what about you?"

"Well," she says, "I'm getting divorced. I have a son who is learning disabled, I'm an inter-faith minister and I also do massage therapy," she reels off. "That's the good stuff," she says. "The bad stuff is that I was back in San Francisco when they had that awful earthquake and, boy, it was incredible. The earth shook like a dog with a rat in its mouth and then suddenly everything went down in a quiet crunch, and one month later to the day I found out I had a thyroid problem and that's when I was told that the best Endo person east of San Francisco is none other than your brother Charlie Fish so I came back East," she says as she dips her head to light her cigarette, "because I got sick. Cancer," she says. "They took my thyroid out at Sloan Kettering—is there any other place?" she laughs. "And then, after, they gave me a whole bunch of stuff that made me so crazy I wanted to die so of course then they had to give me another whole bunch of other stuff to make me normal again, anti-depressants! tranquilizers! sleeping pills! wake-up pills! you name it," she laughs, "only nothing worked until I found your brother Charlie," she says as she exhales.

And as I'm listening I'm thinking how odd that you can't feel another person's suffering and, since she's not really Annie Weiss anymore I really would like to get back to watching Alfred and his girlfriend through the mirror in my compact I'm thinking as I look at her eyes that look like they're completely finished registering anything, What happened to the little girl whose mother wore sequined evening gowns and velvet suits and hats with sequined veils when she took us out to lunch, the little girl who always got straight As and rode horses bareback and spoke French as well as she spoke English, where is she?

"Is your sister Barbara still so ravishingly beautiful?" I ask her carefully, afraid of what she's going to tell me.

"Oh God, *Barbara!* She's alright but in my humble opinion," she says, "she's a real misfit. Three husbands, drugs, booze but you knew she was always a great knitter, so finally she opened up a little knitting shop in Saint Moritz where she's been living since she married husband number one who was a ski instructor. Jane's a grandmother—don't faint! My sister Leslie also had a lot of trouble with booze and drugs so at the moment she's drying out for about the umpteenth time in some hospital up in the Adirondacks and my sister Peggy lives in Palm Beach because her husband, that is her latest husband, husband number four, is a travel agent at one of those fancy hotels down there but don't ask me which one," she chuckles as she takes a deep drag on her cigarette. "My father died two years ago," she says. "My mother's pretty much the same if you know what I mean," she says as her face screws up. "And I'm getting divorced," she says, "from a man named Herby Nelson who married me because he thought I had a lot of money which I didn't have."

"Did you love him?" I say.

"I didn't think about love, he *supported* me," she says.

"I see," I say as I suddenly feel so sad. Life finally breaks your heart I'm thinking as I look at this little dead tattered creature. The struggle to just keep on breathing in and out and then on top of that the second struggle not to be abandoned is something so desperate I'm thinking that it bends a person into lies or numbness or compromises of every kind until finally the spark is done, finished, kaput!

This person standing in front of me came from as close to royalty as anyone I could have imagined as a girl. Now her voice keeps droning on and *on* without any life in it about her marriage to Herby Nelson and about her work as a massage therapist and about her current boyfriend who works in a halfway house near Glassboro whose divorce should be coming through any minute now.

"Come on," she's saying, "another word for motherhood is *terror!* From the instant Rodney was born I did nothing but live in constant terror for his *life!* I couldn't stand it," she's saying, "it drove me crazy, all that worrying!"

"I know," I smile as I'm thinking that the Weiss girls had everything—Money, Brains, and Beauty! and the best education money could buy from the day they put their feet into the best private schools there were plus there was so much glamour around them that you felt glamorous just being in the same room with them and their mother's social secretary Miss Shoehart and their chauffeur Wes who drove the Rolls except of course eventually you find out that there's no such thing as glamour anyhow, just scratch the surface a little and you see how painful it is for everyone to be alive.

We must have been eleven years old when Aunt Lilly took all of us up to Philadelphia in their chauffeur-driven Silver Spur Rolls-Royce to hear Jerome Wildstein who was not only the most famous pianist *in the world* but he was also Uncle Horace and Aunt Lilly's dearest friend. Jerome Wildstein used to sleep in their house which meant nothing to them like the Academy of Music in Philadelphia meant nothing either because they went there all the time but for me it was what Vienna must be like or Rome or Istanbul. Huge golden men held exquisite golden balconies on their shoulders and there was an enormous crystal chandelier in the middle of a golden dome that was made of millions of glittering little crystal balls and even when the house lights dimmed that magnificent thing kept glittering softly up there the whole time with its painted cherubs reclining next to lambs with white painted clouds floating in a soft blue sky and red streamers were flying in the air around half-naked men who were resting beside their golden harps which I couldn't tear my eyes away from because it was all so absolutely magnificent. The Academy of Music on Broad Street in Philadelphia was all gold and ruby velvet with ruby carpets and ruby velvet chairs and as if that wasn't enough . . . there was Aunt Lilly and Uncle Horace's dear friend JEROME WILDSTEIN in a tuxedo sitting in front of an enormous grand piano with the whole Philadelphia Orchestra behind him. The thrill when Maestro Ormandy lifted the baton . . . flicked it furiously . . . then the music . . . and then Jerome Wildstein playing like crazy all by himself.

"Peachy!" I hear Hendella whispering as she comes dashing over, "Alfred Marvel has just arrived!" she's telling me feverishly through a mouth that's so packed with turkey and stuffing that her cheeks are bulging like two fat saddlebags on a camel. "And on top of *that!*" she's whispering, "he's brought *some cockeyed little floozie to my granddaughter Suzie Fish's wedding!* See," she's sputtering, *"Don't you know by now that I know Everything!* I bet he's been seeing this woman for *years!* because they look very comfortable together and I mean *very comfortable!* And let me tell you something else, She's *gorgeous!*" she says. "And does she ever know how to *dress!* Wait till you see the hat and the stockings and those high-heel black alligator *pumps.* She's spending all his money, *Peachy,* Let me tell you, in this life it all comes down to either gorgeous clothes or delicious food be-cause *you can't have both!* Remember, Peachy," she says with her mouth still so crammed full of turkey and stuffing that it looks like she hasn't swallowed in a month, "if he tries to talk to you, *which he will try—don't give him the time of day!* He was nothing but a cheap dirty cheat who I bet was sneaking around behind your back *for years with that little floozie over there—take my word!* and don't forget, while he was spending on her like there was no tomorrow he was so cheap with you that it broke my *heart!* Remember how you had to fight for every little trinket you could wangle out of him while *she* was cashing in with the alligator pumps and the matching alligator handbag and God knows what little bracelets are up those sleeves of hers.

"Remember Peachy," she says, "you can always tell how much a man loves a woman by how deep he'll stick his hands into his pocket and it looks to me like they go pretty deep when it comes to *her* alright because you should get a load of the red wool suit she's wearing, take my word it's a *Chanel* alright," my mother's whispering fiercely through the turkey and the stuffing.

As I'm listening I'm thinking that she can blame him for running around all she wants but how can I? After the baby I'm thinking I had no right to ask anything of anyone because who was I. . . .

"Once upon a time," my mother's whispering, "you were some big success. You were *so gorgeous* you took people's breath away and you made it pay off good by making a *brilliant match* alright," she's whispering, "because, let's face it, Alfred was good looking in those days and he had a lot of money and that's what everybody under the sun hopes their daughters get because that's success of course! *But!*" she says, "he turned out to be some dirty cheat so that in the end you weren't such a big success after all and it wasn't such a brilliant match," she's whispering as she's looking straight at Annie Weiss.

"So, if you ask me," she's saying sort of to Annie Weiss and sort of to me and sort of to herself as she finally starts chewing her saddlebags full of turkey and stuffing, "I was the one who made the brilliant match because when I was young and when I was adorable at least I was smart enough to know it and cash in on it by nabbing a physician who got me out of those damn stinking chicken coops with that horrible smell of ammonia so bad when you first walked in there and took a whiff that you'd start to choke because those damned chickens made sissy and poo and laid their stinking eggs all out of that one rotten little hole," she's telling Annie Weiss. "Let me tell you that was *hell!*" she says as she's chewing. "First it was the heat in there and then that ammonia smell but the worst part was just the thought of touching their scaly little legs. In our heyday," she's telling Annie Weiss, "we had two thousand chickens in one shed alone and we had *eleven sheds!* So of course sometimes when you went in there you could hear right off the bat they were breathing all wrong which meant that they either all had colds or else they all had diarrhea because they used to get epidemics and that's when they'd die all at once because chickens die very fast when something's wrong and since I was the oldest one I was the one who had to walk through there every single morning before I went to school clapping my hands and whistling softly so they'd all automatically get out of my way and the ones that didn't move were the ones that were dead already. You could smell it," she's telling Annie Weiss, "that dead smell mixing with the smell of ammonia the minute you walked in there so I was very glad when I met my husband who got me out of there thank *God!*" she's saying to Annie Weiss whom she doesn't recognize. "Dr. Fish and I had thirty-four wonderful years together and may I tell you he never so much as even *looked* at another woman in his *entire life!* So you tell me who the real success was, me or her?" she's asking Annie Weiss and she turns abruptly and charges off like a dart.

"My *God!*" Annie Weiss says blankly, "she still talks an awful lot doesn't she?"

"Yes," I say as I turn my head and see out of the trail of my eye Alfred kissing Ruthie. Then he hugs her and then he puts his arm around her as he's introducing her to the girlfriend—he *is* indeed very comfortable with the floozie I'm thinking. Hendella's right I'm thinking as I watch Ruthie and the floozie chatting and laughing like they could even become good friends.

And as I'm turning back to Annie Weiss I see Hendella's legs planted wide apart in front of my brother Charlie who's about to catch it now for inviting Alfred and the floozie to Suzie Fish's wedding in the first place. *But it's too late, Hendella,* I'm thinking as I'm staring at Hendella's green-stockinged legs stationed wide apart in front of my brother like two tough sentinels with their arms crossed firmly over their chests in order to protect what's up her skirt—*her Vizzy!* I'm thinking as I watch her begin the whole harangue about Alfred bringing the floozie.

But *Alfred's here Hendella! There's nothing Charlie can do about it now so why are you starting up with him at his daughter's wedding, tell me that!* Couldn't it *wait until tomorrow? So shut up for once in your life* I'm thinking as I see her arms go up and her hands begin flying around and as her mouth starts warming up for another marathon spiel I'm thinking that I have to have some air—*Air! . . . A I R!*

I bolt past Annie Weiss and as I'm rushing toward the kitchen door a little feeling of tension starts up in the pit of my stomach, a little gnawing sort of knot that flies up to my chest and then bursts into a flaming little heat wave that begins roasting my scalp, Dear GOD! What's happening to me *now! Please* let me just get out of this house alive I'm praying as I fly through the kitchen and as I grapple with the back door knob and then let myself out and then run down the four concrete steps into the cool dark peace of the empty yard and hear the screen door bang behind me, my breath which I was having trouble catching comes back into my lungs—*Thank God!* Oh Thank You God I smile as I sit down on the redwood picnic table bench and begin fanning myself with my gold lamé evening bag as a brown wisp of a bug or a leaf or maybe it's a mouse scoots past and then darts behind the trash can.

So, I'm thinking, he's been seeing someone all along alright and it's probably been going on for years just like Hendella said I'm thinking as I watch whatever it is—the little brown wing or mouse or bug—as it comes dashing around the other side of the trash can again and then disappears into the shrubbery. So that's *that,* I'm thinking. Where were my *brains?* Alfred was probably running around with this woman for years. And there must have been one before that and then one before that one, too, probably from the day the baby died.

That's what's dawning on me as I notice a lit window in the basement with a low stone wall around the well which I realize I can stand on and in that way I can see everybody and yet no one will see me so I make my way over to the little ledge, step up on the stones and then lean forward so that I'm spanning the basement well like a human bridge while I'm leaning on the outside of the dining room window. And it works out perfectly! In one fast glance I see Annie Weiss filling her plate and picking off of it as she's meandering slowly past the whole buffet table like she has all year.

Then I shift my eyes a little to the left and I can see Hendella still giving it to Charlie but by now I figure it's probably because he had the nerve to let Rabbi Massengil, with his miniature gold television set dangling down on a long gold chain over his black robe, officiate, especially since the whole TV-Messiah scandal is still so fresh in everybody's mind.

Farther to the left I see Suzie Fish and her husband Arthur Rauch hugging Aunt Hilda and Uncle Archie while Alfred and Ruthie and the girlfriend are talking to Olympia and to Aunt Olivia Krantz whose eyes are beaming joy at Alfred like they're a pair of loving headlights.

Very nice! I'm thinking as I watch Alfred and the floozie shaking hands and smiling with *my new nephew Arthur Rauch! How come?* I'd like to know why they're all turning themselves inside out to welcome *Alfred and that floozie.* What's going on in there? How come my whole family's treating my ex-husband like he's a long lost *hero! Where's a little loyalty* I'm seething, as I'm straining to see all my relatives giving this man, who has probably been running around behind my back with this woman and who he had the gall to dare to bring to my niece's wedding, a *royal welcome!*

While I'm peering in the window of my brother's house like I'm Stella Dallas, my ex-husband is greeting all of my relatives and they're all greeting him like he's a *beloved BROTHER!* I'm thinking as I'm dredging around at the bottom of my pocketbook for my compact.

And as I seize hold of it, as I snap it open and then quickly flash a glance at my face in the light of the street lamp that's just beyond the yard that same tense little feeling begins again in the pit of my stomach as another little heat wave flies up my chest to scald my scalp. So this is *it!* A hot flash, but there's also something a little thrilling about it too. It's my body doing something again and that's always damned exciting. *Good for you old girl!* I whisper to the drawn and haggard face with the white spikes of hair shooting out from the temples that's staring back at me from the mirror in my compact. You've made it through, I whisper, so *bravo Peachy,* Nature or God or whatever they call her these days is at it again with another major plan that's all worked out all the way down to the flowers and the bees and I'm still a part of it which means I'm still a part of *Everything!*

I'm smiling wildly at myself as I twist open my lipstick and put on a dash, flick some blue eye shadow over my lids, dab some pink to my cheeks with the tips of my two middle fingers, powder my nose and chin and then quickly comb my hair before I go back to peering through the window, this time scanning to find Alfred's girlfriend so I can give her a nice good long leisurely look at my convenience. . . . Ah ha! I zero in on her standing between Alfred and Ruthie while they're still all talking to Aunt Livie and to my cousin Olympia Krantz, and as I stand up on my tiptoes on the small stone ledge to be in a better position to see all the way down to her shoes, a wave of relief comes over me because first of all she has a *tremendous behind* that no amount of even the most expensive clothes can do a thing about and secondly, her legs are chunks of rocky muscle on top of black alligator heels and although they're long and tapered at the ankle they're way too thick to ever be called first-class like mine used to be, and as for her hair! It's a beehive of thick lacquered black gristle on top of an extremely pale face which is pretty—granted! But with such *terrible fake* costume earrings that I'm ashamed to have to *look at them* but at least Alfred hasn't given her any particularly expensive stuff *so far* which is a good sign I'm thinking as I'm still stretched out like a bridge over the basement window well while I'm straining to peer around to see whose bag she's carrying. Is it a Hermès or what I'm wondering, as another little twinge of that same little feeling, another little jab begins in the pit of my stomach, shoots up my chest to my scalp and as my face flushes crimson and the perspiration begins I'm thinking that my whole body's working again in a way that I'm bone marrow used to. It's another process I'm going through and I'm used to having these processes because after all up until now I fell off the roof every month like clockwork since I was ten years old and that was a process I not only got used to but I even looked forward to having month in and month out cramps and all. My body made two perfect children, gave birth to them and fed them with its own food for over a year each, which was *a very big deal* and now okay so it's closing shop, which means it must be time for me to maybe have a little *fun!* I'm thinking as I scan around for the handsome and famous neurosurgeon Dr. Anthony Sensacapelli as I begin fanning myself with my evening bag. Not bad I'm thinking as I find him standing all by himself near the pastry section of the buffet table eating an éclair with his fingers and as I'm watching him a little twitch starts kicking up in my vizzy like a couple of frogs in there are jumping around as Alfred turns his face toward the window so that for a moment I can see him perfectly.

In less than a year he looks at least ten years older, he's become so scrawny and peaked. I watch him begin twitching and jerking as he's looking around the room. I was always one of those people who never understood what I lost till it was gone I'm thinking as my eyes stay on him as he walks over to my cousin Naomi Lubin as he's quaffing a handful of potato chips. When they made me leave Vineland High—for what—for stealing a story I never stole—for smoking?—anyhow, I didn't know what was happening to me I'm thinking as I watch him and his girlfriend walking over to the buffet table. I had no idea that day as I walked out the door of Vineland Senior High School that my chances were all over, done and finished forever. All I knew was that my father could never find out about this I'm remembering as my eyes are glued to Alfred—because if he did it would have killed him and no matter what he thought or what anybody thought I never meant him harm, not then or ever, of that I'm sure. If there's one thing I know, it's that in this life all you can blame yourself for is the evil you intended I'm thinking. I watch Alfred pick up a plate and as I'm watching him, as I'm suspended over the basement window well, something in me is suddenly clinging to everything I've lost so that for a moment I feel like one of those magic birds described by Borges who only flies backward not caring where he's going, only where he's been. . . . The day they kicked me out of Vineland High there were no sounds anywhere. Once while I was walking to the bus with all my books and my gym suit and everything that was in my locker I saw a car go by but I didn't hear it. I saw a man walking his dog but I didn't hear him. I saw a woman carrying a bag. I saw a child appear and then disappear into a house but it was all happening without a sound. Nothing jarred the calm that was everywhere. The world outside of school was all stillness with silent climbing vines that had enormous silver leaves shining in the sun. It was all evergreen trees and heather growing wild beside the road and if I wanted I could stop and pick anything I wanted to pick and then I could just stand there looking at it and smelling it for as long as I wanted to stand there sunk deep in all that quiet that was the world of daytime outside of school.

And as I stood breathing in the fragrant air I felt like I was in a dream. For a moment, and it was the kind of moment I never forgot, I saw everything and heard everything—the birds and the Cabbage Whites darting around in the bushes with wild bright sunlight everywhere. And as I stood there dumb with so much happiness I understood what it is that unites everything that lives and breathes with the whole universe yes I was thinking, this is what it's all about—The Immense and Absolute Nothing I was thinking as I stood at the bus stop spellbound as one bus and then another and then another after that came and went while I realized that peace is what freedom is.

The first stop I made before I went home was the Raymond J. Thorpe Free Library on Landis Avenue. In there the air was thin and easy to breathe and the whole place had a gray coolness about it like the stone basement of some ancient church. It was the simpleness of that dark scooped-out shell, the sparseness and the order, but most of all it was the silence which created in me a kind of euphoria. The library was a place where I felt almost unbearably joyful. It was a place to unwind and sit down and look around and then just relish the gift of being alive. In the Raymond J. Thorpe Free Library I felt so excited that I would get dizzy the minute I put my foot inside the rooms with all the books.

The fact that I had just been expelled from high school in my senior year changing the course of my whole life didn't seem to matter then. So *what,* I was thinking. What did I care because what did I know because who knows anything at seventeen? All I knew was that my plan was to go to the Raymond J. Thorpe Free Library every day until the school year was over, sit there and read any book I felt like until the summer came when I would go to summer school to make up my two credits and graduate. It happened that the instant my foot was out the door of that cruelty factory otherwise known as school, the hunger to learn became so overwhelming that I was almost paralyzed by its intensity.

And it was all because of that little nutty art teacher Gladys Danzinger who granted was maybe a little crackers herself but she still did something to all of us that nobody else had ever done and it wasn't just her private seminars on the fine art of bending over or on how to apply makeup or anything like that. It was by whispering in my ear as she clutched my arm, "You, Peachy are an *A-R-T-I-S-T-E!*" that gave me that first real inkling into a truth that was located somewhere in the senses, a truth that once I began to perceive it, I perceived myself.

Thanks to that squat little crackpot with the dyed-black hair and enormous pointy bust like backward ice cream cones, me,

Jessie Nobel, Janie Maxwell, Linda Alter and Emily Goode, became *something* where nothing existed before. Gladys Danzinger was a little bug, nothing more, who changed the way we dressed and spoke and who our friends would be forever. We started listening to different music thanks to her and reading different books and that's what the Raymond J. Thorpe Free Library on Landis Avenue was all about. It was a silent limitless plane where no one could invade. It held possibilities that had no limits and it was solitude and imagination and it was more than even that it was a new part of myself that Mrs. Danzinger told us we must "never compromise," this "gift," she said, "that we had to be worthy of or else we'd lose it," I'm thinking as I'm combing my hair again as I'm leaning against the side of my brother's house.

Of course I wanted to thank her, of course. And of course I also wanted to give her something back for what she had given me, but how could I? How does anybody? Even if they hadn't kicked me out, how does a person ever begin to repay that kind of gift except by running as far away from the person who gave it as you can because the gift is too big to ever begin to repay.

But as I walked out of Vineland High School that day and got on the bus with everything I owned in a brown paper bag and then as I got off the bus in front of the library on the corner of Landis Avenue and Seventh Street, Gladys Danzinger's "vast limitless space" suddenly didn't seem quite so peculiar to me anymore. As I sat down at the long wooden table in the reading room her "great unfathomable sea that was located somewhere in the senses" began to make a bit more sense.

Youth was optimism. It was high ideals and altruism and it was secretly believing that I had been promised a lucky life as the memory of the tiny mirrored fitting room at Wanamaker's department store floats up complete with Hendella snapping at everyone about my wedding dress and the nervous salesgirls who kept bringing the wrong shoes while she kept nipping on Scotch from a little brown medicine bottle as she fanned herself with one of those bridal magazines. . . .

I carried white gardenias and I had lilies of the valley in my hair as I walked down the aisle on my brother Charlie's arm because Leo Fish never made it into the spring that year.

Enough! Do you hear! I've had enough of your damn lousy silences I'm thinking. Did you think in ten million years that I could have *ever ever meant* to do something so terrible to you that I can't bear to even think about you anymore? *Come on,* I'm whispering in the dark of my brother Charlie's yard in the middle of the night. Could I, who loved you so much, have *ever E V E R meant to do you so much harm?* I'm whispering at the moon as the tears begin boiling up.

Maybe Hendella should have kept her mouth shut for once in her life about the trouble I had in school that day because it was she, not I, who got you all steamed up so go blame *her* for a change, she knew all about your high blood pressure better than anyone, all I did was write a story on a bus for a twelfth-grade English class. That's right, I said *"write"* not *"steal"*.

And as I'm wiping my nose on the back of my hand that little thing goes dashing by again. That little brown gossamer wing or else it's a little squirrel, or maybe it's a chipmunk or who knows, maybe it's the soul of one of the countless gerbils or dogs or hamsters or cats or rabbits that came into our home over all those years I'm thinking as my cousin Naomi Lubin comes up to the dining room window so close that I could touch her if the window wasn't locked with a storm window over it. Naomi Fish with her thick black curly hair and her enormous boobs bobbing around without a bra under her Mexican peasant blouse as she danced wildly at my wedding with Norman Lubin while her hips jiggled and her thighs swirled around like giant Dairy Queens. Once when I was little I saw her naked at the seashore and I was so dazzled by her breasts, I was so stunned by those huge pyramids soaring out from the middle of her chest, those big perfect mountains of sculptured flesh with those big pink-brown nipples looking up to God and after that my cousin Naomi Fish became exquisite in my eyes even with her high-pitched screechy voice and the way she talked so fast you couldn't understand her half the time and all that thick black kinky hair. What people go through I'm thinking and that they *endure!* That's what's so amazing. *That they endure!*

Her husband Norman Lubin was the youngest professor of English at the University of Pennsylvania when he threw himself under the subway because he didn't get tenure. That was the story they told but my brother Charlie said it was morphine I'm thinking as I see Naomi roaring with laughter, her mouth full of half-chewed brisket as she throws her head back in hysterics at something Loretta's telling her. There must be some universal law that insists on healing and Naomi Lubin makes me hate how strong it is I'm thinking as I'm peering at her through the storm window because six months after Norman Lubin died she married Barney Grebler, a psychiatrist from South Orange who published a bestselling diet book titled *Binging on Your Guilt*. Then she had two more sons and now she's laughing and dancing and eating her head off while I've never come out from under the rock where I buried myself, I'm still a bug with glossy little wings and little thin front legs that rub against each other to make the only music I ever hear out here while she's in there laughing and eating I'm thinking as I see that little gossamer wing shoot by again and then dash into the bushes.

How come she's doing so great I'm wondering while I scuttle around on the bottom of the world with all the other weird little things that run in panic if God forbid we see a beam of brightness to send us frightened racing racing back and forth, our arms flying up to shield our eyes because we dare not look at anything that light and white because the brightness brings us terror as we go racing back and forth, back and forth across the floor of time, in all our darkness. We only want the darkness because it's safe and sound that way and all sealed up and done. No more nights when I used to lie in bed all cozy and warm under my Egyptian sheets and goose-down blankets while the cars outside made lazy jelly shadows all along the ceiling coming and going in slow motion like some enormous joyful heartbeat. But I'm not like that. I never healed like my cousin Naomi Lubin, not me, I'm still one of those weird little things that's still scuttling across the floor of time with my arms still up to cover my eyes in case there's God forbid one tiny beam of light while I keep begging them to please just go away leave me alone I keep telling them and whatever they do I tell them, please, just don't lift the rock I'm thinking as I'm dredging around in my pocketbook for my Kleenex so I can blow my nose.

"Long time no see," I hear a voice behind me rumble. And as I turn I find. . . . Alfred Baruch Marvel.

"Still wearing that perfume that smells like dirty pussy," he says as a big grin breaks out across his face. And as he bends to kiss me and at the same time as he takes my hand I'm thinking *Courage, Peachy!*

Remember, I'm telling myself, *God hates cowards! Guts and brains! That's what you're made of, remember,* I'm thinking, *God didn't give you fear! God gave you a strong mind and a strong will and that's who you are,* I'm telling myself as I feel my legs begin to buckle and my hands start trembling as I hear myself saying, "It's been a long time, Alfred," as I stare at a face that's as familiar to me as the sight of my own hands that I've been looking at and seeing since the first day of my life.

"You look *great!*" he says while we're still shaking hands. "Is that a tan I see? Have you been away with someone? A man?" he says as we keep shaking hands like two idiots.

I look great I'm thinking. Who is he kidding? Have I been away with a man?

Hm—m-m-m, I'm thinking, maybe just to see if he still cares anymore, maybe I should tell him that I've been away with *the* Manuel Zot, just to see his reaction, maybe I should tell him that Manuel Zot and I spent the last few months up in Cambridge living in a little apartment overlooking the Charles River and besides helping out with Manuel's new manuscript, reading it and giving my suggestions, maybe I should tell him we were taking long strolls in the evenings and hot baths together and sipping red wine out of the same glass in front of a roaring fire while our eyes were locked and our hands held onto each other. Except I better not say that because he'd know in one minute flat that that was what we used to do, me and Alfred with so much enormous need for each other that it used to scare the daylights out of both of us and since he's so damn smart he'd also know in one minute flat from having read Zot's books that Manuel Zot is someone who could never be overwhelmed by love, not the way that Alfred could. Zot was missing that capacity I'm thinking as I look at this man who, even when I used to lie to make myself look better to him which I did a lot, never criticized me. He always kind of understood what I was up to and he'd let it go so that everything I did was okay, everything I said was funny, everything I wore was smart even when it wasn't, he even thought I was a knockout which I never was. I was a dog if you ask me but he never noticed which is maybe what love is all about.

How sad it is to realize all this now the same as it's sad to realize that he hasn't noticed now that I've become invisible but maybe it's just the light out here or maybe he's saying I look great for old time's sake, or maybe he's just trying to be polite, or maybe, I'm thinking, he's being sarcastic, or maybe I look so bad and he's so shocked to see it that he has to say something— anything because sometimes when I see someone wearing something so ugly that it takes my breath away, for some odd reason I have to mention how fabulous I think it is. And not because I'm insincere but because I'm so stunned at how hideous it is that I have to comment and luckily it comes out in a kindly way I'm thinking as his girlfriend appears out of the shadows advancing carefully to keep tabs on her prize.

And as she advances, out of the trail of my eye I see that same little brown gossamer creature zooming by again.

What is it? I'm thinking. Could it be the soul of the little girl we buried next to Leo Fish or maybe it's old Leo Fish himself, or maybe it's a little feather or a piece of cellophane the wind is pushing over toward the redwood picnic table, I can't be sure as I look at Alfred's pinched face with his red straggly sage-brush hair that's getting gray around the temples, his bloodshot sky-blue eyes with bags under them, his Big Mac lips and his same old earthquake tremor and neck jerk like he's doing the conga as he's standing in front of me making odd small talk because he doesn't know what else to do, because who on earth ever says out loud what he's really thinking. Like how could I ever begin to tell him that one day I felt like I didn't deserve being married to him anymore the same as I didn't deserve anything—the house I loved so much, a new piano or even a little pair of diamond studs. How could I tell him that after the baby died it was all over for me I'm thinking as we're still shaking hands. I didn't deserve to go to the beach with him in the summers anymore like I didn't deserve to go out to Hong Kong with him on any of those lavish business trips where you can buy all the cameras and wristwatches and all the fabulous shoes and pocketbooks you want because I was the one who held onto the steering wheel. So no, I'm thinking as I look at his face and then start scanning it all over again still looking to see if there's any forgiveness in it anywhere for me, no, I'm thinking, better to just shut up and leave him out here with his girlfriend. Go inside, I tell myself, get a bite to eat with Ruthie and Hendella and just be glad the girlfriend doesn't bring him pain or remind him of it all the time the way I do. He's found some peace so it figures that of course he'd fall in love I'm thinking as I'm trying to shore myself up in order to make the break with the feel of Alfred's hand again. . . .

Involuntary manslaughter, that's what they called it. That's what the policeman said before anyone came I'm thinking as I'm staring at Alfred's shoes. She was in another room away from me. I was all alone and couldn't smoke because they said it was regulations. That's when the other one asked me if we were Catholic. Last rites he said and I said is the baby okay because maybe I was wrong but all he answered was to ask again if we were Catholic and then after that they fed me chicken soup and Cokes.

I groped through all those twigs and thorns in braille I'm thinking as I stare at Alfred's trousers, but I didn't see or feel a thing for God how long the healing takes. And still to this day it starts to itch so much right before it rains all across my forehead where I was smashed up pretty bad myself and then I have to scratch so hard where they sewed it up that I swear I could tear it open just from scratching and then I'll be right back out there beside that tree again or else I would dream the same dream night after night about the three of us, me and the baby and

Alfred, we were going on a holiday, the air was always new summer sweet and there was always the same laughing song that had no words as the three of us were holding hands and singing till black birds flew out all across a brand-new purple dawn and that's when I'd wake up and feel myself starting to sink all over again and that's also when I knew that no matter how much you love someone you could never stay married with a noose like that around your neck.

Impossible, I'm thinking, as I feel his grip tightening on my hand.

"Peachy," he says, as he's holding me in a vise by now with his entire body strength, "this is Ellen Keshevsky," he says as he keeps tightening his grip on me.

"Ellen," he says, "this is my wife" he says as he keeps tightening his grip even more to keep me from darting off which he knows is exactly what I want to do.

If I only were an iguana I'd have bitten off my tail twenty thousand times by now just to get out of this damn situation I think as I nod to this beautiful young woman who can't be more than twenty-eight or twenty-nine years old. Oh God! Alfred, how can you do a thing like this to Ruthie. But then I guess after what we've been through it's not so terrible I'm thinking as he puts his arm around the woman standing next to him and gives her a little squeeze as he pulls her closer.

"Ellen," he says, "is the new chief of obstetrics and gynecology at South East Regional Hospital and I have the honor of being her date tonight because her handsome husband is still in the hospital recovering from back surgery."

. . . .
. . . .
. . . .

Jerk! Peachy, I'm thinking.

Idiot!

Dope!

Lunatic!

What's *wrong with you?* I'm thinking as we shake hands and smile wildly at each other.

Wow! Not bad! This divine creature is the chief of obstetrics and gynecology and probably a full professor of medicine besides. And notice how charming and sweet she is with no airs about her at all. And on top of that she's *married*. And she doesn't wear expensive jewelry which is very interesting. Her earrings are plain little department store junk that comes on a white card and her pearls are so fake that no one has to bite them to know they're big fat plastic nothings. It's all different these days I mean about what accomplishment looks like. In my day I'm thinking as we keep smiling and shaking hands, it was how may doodads, pins and bracelets you could finagle out of your husband so that your friends would see that someone thought something of you and as we keep shaking hands and smiling at each other my spirits soar because she's married to someone else. "Ellen went to Radcliffe so she and Ruthie have plenty to talk about," Alfred says.

Hm—m-m-m, not bad I'm thinking. "I see," I say.

Then we smile and nod some more and begin saying all the right things to each other and then as we start to shake hands again, Alfred says, "So here we are, Peachy," and with that she turns and starts walking back to the house.

Oh God! please dear *God, please!* I'm thinking as the back door flies open and two caterers come out hauling a can of trash.

Thank you God for giving me this extra minute to collect myself I'm thinking as the blaring music from the combo in the living room fills the whole backyard so that for one moment it feels like Alfred and I are back again shopping at the Gap.

"So," he says, "I was just saying, here we are with a whole lifetime on our shoulders."

"Yes," I say as I'm thinking, Dear God, *please!* I want him *back!*

You can keep Manuel Zot. Oh, not that I ever imagined anything much could have ever happened between the two of us. Maybe for a night or two or something along those lines, of course, because let's face it, he was the only man whoever gave me even a dirty look since Alfred and I split up and God knows a lot of women would have snapped that up—a famous writer, a professor, a handsome, dashing, fabulous celebrity with a ton of money and all of that, so why did I run out of there, why didn't I "stick around" like he wanted me to?

Because when you get right down to it, was Manuel Zot one jot smarter than Alfred Marvel? No!

Was Manuel Zot even in the same *class* as far as looks and style are concerned?

Absolutely not!

Was Manuel Zot kind like Alfred is? Not at all I'm thinking or

Manuel Zot wouldn't have tortured me with exposing all the contents of my pocketbook the way he did. That was a real tip-off because couldn't he see how humiliated I was while I was struggling?

Alfred would have *never* done a thing like that because Alfred has a sweetness and I'm used to that kind of sweetness and my eyes well up from remembering Alfred long ago when he was young.

"So you're not going to tell me anything about your suntan?" he says.

"Because I'm not suntanned," I answer as I'm thinking that I knew Alfred when he was twenty-two years old and he knew me when I was *eighteen!*

He had a red Pontiac convertible. We once put the top down in a snowstorm and then drove all the way to where my friend Riva Robinson lived with that parrot she used to have that started laying eggs when it was thirty-one years old back when all my guilt was coming straight from Leo Fish. Well, I've come a long way guiltwise, haven't I? So maybe the question I have to finally figure out the answer to is where do I find a little Grace. That's the question I'm thinking as I look at Alfred's wrinkled, soft blue eyes.

Except maybe there just isn't any, or maybe Grace is too big or too elusive or maybe it's just not in the cards for me I'm thinking as I look at Alfred's thick red hand. It's not like he's even my husband I'm thinking. It's more like he's a blood relative who knew everyone, my grandmother and all my aunts and uncles and my grandfather and old Leo Fish.

There's so much sadness in remembering Alfred when he was young because it's as though that person vanished without a trace except for that wildness he always had, his motorcycle and those black leather pants he wore without any underwear, same as Albert Einstein used to wear black leather pants and no underwear so Einstein must have also had a wildness and so must that shrink of his . . . that low-life Corbin Segal who also used to wear black leather pants. . . .

"So how's your mother," he asks.

"Didn't you see her inside?" I say.

"I saw her but we didn't get a chance to talk. Is she fine?" he says.

. . . I was just eighteen I'm thinking and he was twenty-two. He had no gray hair back then, no jowls, no bags under his eyes and nothing weary in his face.

He would never take no for an answer. I tried to get away from him a couple of times because for me even then there was never Grace, even then I had such a heavy load to carry but he just kept coming back and coming back and coming back like a dog that had a shoe in his mouth, tenacious, he wouldn't let go.

I loved him because he was good, you could see it all over him and I was always drawn to that, in fact, I think it's the hidden secret to sex appeal.

. . . "I still don't understand why you want this divorce," he's saying. "Granted, every day wasn't perfect but we had a beautiful house. We had two Mercedes and we could go to any restaurant we wanted any time we felt like it and aside from that," he's saying, "I'd rather see all that money going to Ruthie instead of to that shark attorney of yours, Sid Sheidell with that floppy leg he's got and that face that looks like somebody stepped on it and all that gold jewelry he wears like he's some kind of gangster gigolo. That slime is taking you to the cleaners, Peachy. But there isn't a whole lot I can do about it is there? I just don't understand—that's all. I thought we were happy," he says. "We were happy—weren't we? I was happy so it's odd to think that I was happy all by myself."

"It wasn't that we weren't happy," I say. "*Of course* we were happy!"

"So, Peachy, what was the problem? Think about how many years it took to get this way."

"What way?"

"Comfortable."

"Comfortable?"

"Comfortable!"

"What do you mean?"

"I mean *comfortable!* I mean not being afraid of losing each other anymore. I mean being able to say what you honestly think, I mean finally taking my shoes off because I know there's no place else to go that's any better. I mean being able to tell you anything and know you'll take it the right way.

"It used to be so great at night," he says.

"What was?"

"Just leaning up against you."

"But Alfred—what about *Grace?*"

"What Grace?" he asks.

"Grace!"

"Don't worry about Grace," he says. "It's too big a thing. Just be grateful for being comfortable," he says. "Comfortable is finally realizing that what you are can never be destroyed or replaced because you know you're part of the whole eternal picture like Nancy is. She's there. No one can ever replace her and she can never be destroyed. She, like the rest of us, was always there and she, like the rest of us, will always *be* there because nothing that ever was can be annihilated. That's what I mean by being comfortable. It's finding our places in the universe."

"That crazy shrink of yours said Grace was to be found in making a lot of money."

"You know," he says, "you were off your rocker when it came to Corbin Segal. I want you to know that," Alfred says. "Corbin was a little fat harmless egomaniac—big deal in the scheme of things and who knows, maybe Grace *is* to be found in making a lot of money.

"So tell me, where did you get the suntan? What's his name?"

Looks like he still wants to play that same old game, looks like human nature never changes but if that's what he wants let's see if I still have my same old skill I'm thinking as I start warming up.

"Well," I say, "if you must know, I do have to admit that when I took Ruthie up to school I did have the unexpected pleasure of meeting Manuel Zot. You know, *the* Manuel Zot," I say very slowly to let the name sink in, "who I have to say in all modesty was very taken with me."

I notice his eyes widening and a little red flush coming into his cheeks.

"So naturally, when he invited me out a little later for a cup of coffee," I go on calmly, confident now that I have the first round completely under control, "of course I went because why not? After all I was tasting a little bit of freedom for the first time in my life—right? And I have to admit in all honesty that it was pretty interesting because after all, Manuel Zot is a very fascinating man. He's brilliant, charming, not bad looking if you like the type, which is tall, thin, dark, and a little on the wild coyote side with very sharp wolf family features who I have to admit again, could not, and I mean *could not* take his eyes off me for a single second."

I'm hoping this information will fire him into the old seething jealousy I always used to be able to pull out of him without half trying.

"I'm not saying he was spellbound, Alfred, don't misunderstand," I continue, "but I do have to admit that he was smitten with me to say the least."

"And he stiffed you for the check—right?"

"Yes," I say. "How did you know?"

How did he know? Because he always knows . . . that's the damned eerie part.

He has an antenna, did I forget that! Did I forget how smart and shrewd he is and did I forget also that it's very hard to pull anything over on "The Swami Salami" as we used to call him back in the old days because he was always one step ahead like, for instance, did I forget what it was like to play cards with him and how a little innocent game of gin turned him into a killer who was all brains and cunning, the shifty looks as he took his pick, the calculations going on, scanning my face as I took my pick, the way he slipped a gin or a blitz in on me from out of nowhere. You never know a man till you play cards with him I'm thinking.

Or give him his daily vitamins. The way he'd put out his hand every morning while he kept reading the paper while I'd put a bunch of pills into it and he'd just swallow them in one fast gulp without a glance except one day when we ran out of B-Complex and without even looking, while he was still reading the paper he simply said, "So where is my B?" I never got over that I'm thinking, and I never will.

"You want to know how I know?" Alfred leers at me. "Because all those intellectuals, all those world-class brains are the biggest freeloaders that ever lived or *breathed*. I wouldn't be one bit surprised if he even tried to get you into bed. And why not," he says, as he's getting all steamed up, "it's free! No strings! No credit card! No life insurance policy, Peachy, just a good fast roll and then some long-winded conversation about how great he is and then so long, see you around and *oops*, I'm sorry, but I forgot my wallet so if you don't mind paying the bill. . . . I'm not impressed—Sorry!" he's almost yelling as I hear a tapping on the window.

And as I turn away from him to look I see Hendella glaring at me with a menacing scowl all over her face as she begins motioning me to come into the house *this minute!* I should get away from Alfred *now!* she's motioning me, unless of course he has marriage on his mind, in which case she's indicating to me by holding her wedding ring finger up and then pointing to where the ring belongs, then *of course,* her lips are going a mile a minute, I should listen to him *with both ears* she's indicating as she's pulling her ears out to make sure I understand.

. . . And furthermore he's saying, "In the end you'll either be alone or else, eventually, you'll wind up with someone exactly like me. And then the only person who will have profited by all this will be that stinking shark Sid Sheidell and you know how I feel about that fucking bloodsucker," he says as the twitching and the neck jerks begin as his jaw starts jumping around.

"So what I'm thinking," he says, "since you've never been to Israel," he says as a big grin breaks out again across his face that's so huge you can see all his molars, "and since it is September," he says, "which means the High Holidays are coming up in a week or so, why don't we go to Israel and talk everything over before we sign the final papers.

"We can leave from Boston," he says. "That way we can have dinner with Ruthie at the Ritz the night before we leave. Nothing but the *best!*" he's saying as the sinking feeling begins again in the pit of my stomach.

. . . Hold on a minute I'm thinking. Alfred, you haven't answered my question about *Grace!*. . . You don't understand! At the moment I don't feel like discussing Sid Sheidell or the

High Holidays or a fabulous trip with "nothing but the *best!*" I feel like discussing *G R A C E!* Alfred, *G R A C E!* I'm thinking as the tapping on the window starts again, only this time faster. And as I look over this time Hendella's glaring at me with both her hands on her hips. Her mouth doesn't start till she sees she's got my full attention, then up comes one hand to flag me in while at the same time a finger from the other hand goes directly to her lips to indicate to me that I should *keep my big mouth shut* until we have a little conversation.

. . . *Hendella! You're all wet about everything and you always were so would you please just shut up for once in your life* I glare at her as the little brown gossamer wing darts past the trash can again on its trip around to the other side of the house.

Once when Alfred was young I remember as I glance down at his shoes again, he gave his watch to a Gypsy girl who had a little beggar brother because she was so beautiful that he wanted to give her all the money in his pockets plus his watch and his two bus tokens back then when he was so good-looking I'm thinking, with all that red shaggy hair and how straight he was and tall, he was my real mother—his armpit was my hiding place and my shelter. He was my best friend, I trusted him and I loved his feel and I loved to kiss him and hug him and it was really good with that big thing of his before the baby died I'm thinking as the little brown wing comes scooting around the house, this time from the other side. . . .

What is it? I'm thinking.

What can it be? I squint in the dim light of my brother's back yard in an effort to get a better glimpse. . . .

Who are you? I whisper. Are you a little leaf the wind is pushing or are you a tiny scurrying creature or a bug?

It's dark out here so it's really hard to tell without my glasses on I'm thinking as it scoots over toward the barbecue and then back real fast into the bushes near the garage.

. . . Are you Nancy I'm wondering or are you the soul of old Leo Fish that day with his thumb and forefinger making a circle with the other three fingers straight up to make the three-ring sign as he smiled to Hendella and me and then he died or are you just a little bit of milkweed floating with no history at all through an astonishingly beautiful night I'm wondering as it goes flying over to the back door steps, then over to the trash cans again and then round and round in front of the redwood picnic table as if it's caught on the wind that's driving it wildly through the air as it's swirling upwards until it lands directly on Alfred's right shoulder where it stops for a minute to catch the little flecks of dust that are glistening in the light of the street lamp so that for just that moment it looks like a luminous little grasshopper with wonderful shimmering wings, or like a little silver moth, or maybe it's more like the little sparkling diamond in the ring my brother Charlie gave me the night before he married Loretta Finkel.

And as I put my hand up to touch it, as I'm groping toward it, dazzled for a moment by the brilliance of its light I understand its message.

Forgive, Forgive, Forgive, it's saying, *so that you can go on loving.*

And as I turn around and look up at the zillion stars that dot the sky like chains of blazing lights, and then as I look over at the diamond dust that's swirling all around the lamp light in the night, I hear it whispering that the real miracle is that we were ever here at all. *My God*, it's whispering, *weren't we lucky that we were even here at all.*